# HARLEQUIN®
## *Presents*

Welcome to this month's collection of Harlequin Presents! At this festive time of year, why not bring some extra sparkle and passion to your life by relaxing with our brilliant books! For all of you who've been dying to read the next installment of THE ROYAL HOUSE OF NIROLI, the time has come! Robyn Donald continues the series with *The Prince's Forbidden Virgin,* where Rosa and Max struggle with their mutual—but dangerous—desire, until the truth about a scandal from the past may set them free.

Also this month, Julia James brings you *Bedded, or Wedded?* Lissa's life has too many complications, but she just can't resist ruthless Xavier's dark, lethal sexuality. In *The Greek Tycoon's Pregnant Wife* by Anne Mather, Demetri needs an heir, but before he divorces Jane, he'll make love to her one last time. In *The Demetrios Bridal Bargain* by Kim Lawrence, Mathieu wants a wife of convenience, and taming wild Rose into the marital bed will be his pleasure! Sharon Kendrick brings you *Italian Boss, Housekeeper Bride,* where Raffaele chooses his mousy housekeeper, Natasha, to be his pretend fiancée! If you need some help getting in the holiday mood, be sure not to miss the next two books! In *The Italian Billionaire's Christmas Miracle* by Catherine Spencer, Domenico knows unworldly Arlene isn't mistress material, but might she be suitable as his wife? And in *His Christmas Bride* by Helen Brooks, Zak is determined to claim vulnerable Blossom as his bride—by Christmas! Finally, fabulous new author Jennie Lucas brings you *The Greek Billionaire's Baby Revenge,* in which Nikos is furious when he discovers Anna's taken his son, so he vows to possess Anna and make her learn who's boss! Happy reading, and happy holidays from Harlequin Presents!

## In Bed WITH THE Boss

*Chosen by him for business,
taken by him for pleasure…*

A classic collection of office romances from
Harlequin Presents, by your favorite authors.

Look out for more, coming soon!

# Sharon Kendrick

## ITALIAN BOSS, HOUSEKEEPER BRIDE

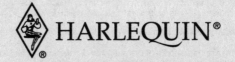

IN Bed WITH THE Boss

HARLEQUIN®

TORONTO • NEW YORK • LONDON
AMSTERDAM • PARIS • SYDNEY • HAMBURG
STOCKHOLM • ATHENS • TOKYO • MILAN • MADRID
PRAGUE • WARSAW • BUDAPEST • AUCKLAND

ISBN-13: 978-0-373-23451-6
ISBN-10:     0-373-23451-1

ITALIAN BOSS, HOUSEKEEPER BRIDE

First North American Publication 2007.

Copyright © 2007 by Sharon Kendrick.

www.eHarlequin.com

Printed in U.S.A.

All about the author...
*Sharon Kendrick*

When I was told off as a child for making up stories, little did I know that one day I'd earn my living by writing them!

To the horror of my parents, I left school at sixteen and did a bewildering variety of jobs: I was a London DJ (in the now-trendy Primrose Hill!), a decorator and a singer. After that, I became a cook, a photographer and eventually a nurse. I waitressed in the South of France, drove an ambulance in Australia and saw lots of beautiful sights, but could never settle down. Everywhere I went, I felt like a square peg—until one day I started writing again, and then everything just fell into place.

Today, I have the best job in the world—writing passionate romances for Harlequin. I like writing stories that are sexy and fast-paced, yet packed full of emotion—stories that readers will identify with, and laugh and cry along with.

My interests are many and varied: chocolate and music, fresh flowers and bubble baths, films and cooking—and trying to keep my home from looking as if someone's burgled it! Simple pleasures—you can't beat them!

I live in Winchester, and regularly visit London and Paris. Oh, and I love hearing from my readers all over the world...so I think it's over to you!

With warmest wishes,

Sharon Kendrick (www.sharonkendrick.com)

To Bryony Green, the best editor in the world!

# CHAPTER ONE

NATASHA didn't have to see his face to know something was wrong.

She could tell from the slamming of the door and the heavy footfalls in the hall. From the momentary hesitation which was not like Raffaele at all. The barely muffled curse; some Italian expletive, she thought. She listened while he hung his suit jacket up in the hall and heard him go into his study. Then silence—and something very much like fear stirred within her and she didn't understand why.

He had been away to America—where he owned real-estate on both the east and west coast—and whenever he returned from a trip he always came to find her. To ask her how she'd been. How Sam was.

Sometimes, if he was flying by commercial rather than private jet, he would even remember to bring the child some soft toy or game that he'd bought at the airport. Once she had seen him remove a shiny gold box of perfume from his briefcase, and her heart had begun to thud with a ridiculous excitement. But she had never seen it again.

The scent had not been destined for Natasha. Presumably it had gone to the leggy super-model he had been seeing at the time—the one who'd always used to leave a stocking or a scarf behind in the bathroom, like some territorial trophy, marking out her pitch.

The study was still ominously silent, and Natasha began making a pot of mega-strong coffee—just as Raffaele had taught her to when she'd first gone to work for him. Wasn't it crazy how memories could stay stuck fast in your head, even though they meant nothing? Natasha could still remember the shiver she'd felt as he'd bent close to her, too close for her comfort— though, not, it had seemed, for his. He had been too intent on showing her what to do to notice the mousy-looking woman at his side.

His voice had dipped, like soft velvet under-pinned with steel. 'In Italy we say that the coffee should look like ink and taste like heaven. Very strong and very dark—like the best kind of man. You understand? *Capisci?*'

And the black eyes had glittered at her in mocking question, as if it amused him that a woman should need to be taught how to make coffee.

But she had. Oh, she had. Back then she had needed teaching about pretty much everything that someone like Raffaele took for granted. While he was used to only the very best, she'd always been the kind of person who usually spooned instant out of a jar—until the time had come when she'd had barely enough money to buy any. Just thinking about the mess she had found herself in still had the power to make her tremble with apprehension. She never wanted to go back there—to those days of hunger and uncertainty and real fear—to before Raffaele had stepped in to save her.

*Was that why she'd put him on a pedestal ever since?*

Natasha placed the coffee and cup on the tray, along with two of the small almond biscuits which were Raffaele's favourites. She had learnt how to make those, too, from the Italian cookbook he had bought her one Christmas.

Then she checked her appearance in the kitchen mirror, just as any employee would do before going in to see their boss—even if they didn't happen to live in the same house, as Natasha did.

She would do. Her pale brown hair was neat, her dress carefully ironed and her features unadorned by make-up. She looked efficient and unthreatening. The way she liked it.

Going bare-faced was a habit she'd gotten into when Sam was a baby, when she'd been terrified of being judged by other people more than she already had been. She had wanted to send out the message that being a struggling single mother didn't mean she was sexually available.

Besides, Natasha had learnt that it was easier if you kept things simple. There were advantages to almost everything in life—it all boiled down to your attitude. No make-up meant more time in the morning—just as tying her hair back did. She looked just what she hoped she was—a respected and respectable member of Raffaele's staff.

'Natasha!'

She heard his peremptory summons couched in the distinctively accented voice as it carried down to the basement. Hastily, she picked up the tray and carried it upstairs to his study, but in the doorway she paused, her attention caught and arrested by the sight of him. Natasha frowned. Her instinct had been right—there *was* something wrong.

Raffaele de Feretti. Billionaire. Bachelor. Boss. And the man she had quietly loved from almost since the first time she'd set eyes on him. But who wouldn't love him? *Not* loving him would have presented a greater challenge— despite his arrogance and that disdainful air he had sometimes, when he wasn't really listening to what you said.

He hadn't heard her now and was standing with his back to her, gazing out onto the drenched garden at the centre of the London square, where raindrops dripped down the trees like a woman's tears.

Today the garden was deserted, but on fine days you could see nannies with their boisterous young charges running around the paths to the tiny playground section at the far end. Or mothers with prams, before they went back to work—as many of the mothers around this affluent part of the city seemed to do whether it was because they needed the variety or because they wanted the independence. Natasha could never quite work it out. She used to think that it would be bliss not to *have* to work, but that was probably because the option had never been open to her.

Natasha used to take Sam to the garden when

he was younger—feeling very privileged to be able to do so, but slightly nervous, too, as if someone was about to move her on, to tell her she had no right to be there. Her son, of course, had been unaware of the exclusive location of his playground, but every time her beloved little boy had patted his bucket and squealed with delight as sand flew out, Natasha had thanked a benevolent fate for bringing Raffaele de Feretti into her life.

'Raffaele?' she said quietly.

But Raffaele didn't look round. Not even when she put the tray down on his desk with a little clatter. His tall, lean body just remained there—as unmoving as a statue and as silent as a rock—and there was something so *perturbing* and so *alien* about his stance that Natasha cleared her throat.

'Raffaele?' she prompted again.

Her soft English accent filtered into his fractured thoughts and slowly Raffaele turned round, his eyes taking in her familiar face and the gentle concern in her eyes. He sighed. Natasha. As ever-present and unthreatening as the air he breathed. He frowned, brought back to the present with a jolt. He had been miles away. 'What is it?'

'I've brought you your coffee,'

Coffee? Had he asked for any? Probably not—but he could certainly do with some. How like her to guess. He nodded, gesturing for her to pour some and then he sat down in the leather chair at his desk, running his fingertips along the dark rasp of his jaw, the way he always did when something was on his mind. It was usually a high-profile takeover of some big company, but today it happened to be something much bigger. His mouth hardened—because unlike corporate affairs, which he could practically deal with in his sleep, this particular problem was something he usually steered clear of. The personal.

'Has anyone called this morning?' he demanded.

'Not a soul.'

'No press?'

'No.' The tabloids had upped the ante ever since a reality-TV star had claimed that Raffaele had bedded her in a '*Five Times a Night!*' romp, when he had barely met the woman. The matter was currently in the hands of his lawyers, and just the thought of it made Natasha feel quite sick, even though she knew it wasn't true. She tried a joke, to try to help ease that terrible tension which was tightening the face she knew so well. 'Well, no *visible* press—I guess, there could always be a couple of reporters hiding in the bushes. It's happened before!'

But he didn't laugh. 'You've been in the whole time?'

Natasha nodded. 'Except when I dropped Sam off at school, of course—but I was back by nine-thirty.' Her mouth softened with concern. This close, she could see he looked somehow *different*. His brilliant black eyes were shadowed and the tiny lines which fanned outwards from them seemed somehow more pronounced. As if he had gone without sleep while he'd been away. 'Why? Were you expecting someone?'

Not exactly *expecting*—because that might imply that he had invited someone, and there had categorically been no invitation issued. Raffaele gave a small shake of his head. He was a man who did not give his trust easily—his suspicions had been fuelled by a lifetime of mixing with people who wanted something from him. Sex or money or power—the magical trinity which he had in spades. With Natasha he had come pretty close to implicit trust—but he was still aware of the dangers of confiding in others except when absolutely necessary.

The more people you told, the weaker you became. Because knowledge was power—and, surely, this quiet Englishwoman already knew far too much about how he lived his life. For now, he had her loyalty, because she owed him a great debt—but what if greed reared its ugly head and persuaded her to sell out, as he had seen happen so many times in the past? What if she discovered that she could make enough to keep her in comfort for many years if she sold her story to the papers, who were always hungry to find out more about him?

'No, Natasha—I wasn't expecting anyone,' he said, with blunt honesty.

'You're back from America early.'

'I haven't been in America. I flew to Italy, instead.'

'Oh? Any special reason?' She pushed the sugar towards him, knowing that she was being unusually persistent—but she had never seen him look quite so troubled before.

'It doesn't matter.'

But, because she loved him, Natasha chose to ignore the sudden dark, repressive tone of his voice. 'Something's wrong—isn't it, Raffaele?'

Inexplicably, he felt the flicker of temptation for one brief moment, before his mouth curved with an aristocratic disdain he rarely used on her. 'It is not your place to ask me such a question,' he answered coolly. 'You know that.'

Yes, she knew that—and mainly she accepted it. Just as she accepted so many other things about his life. Like the women who sometimes shared his bed, who would wander down to breakfast in the morning, all tousle-haired and pink-cheeked, long after he had left for the City. They would giggle as they demanded she make them French toast and orange juice and Natasha's jealous heart would break into a thousand pieces.

It was true that there hadn't been any of those *interlopers* for some time—in fact, he was probably gearing up for another any day now. Maybe *that* was what was bugging him? Was some woman giving *him* the runaround, for once—instead of the other way round? In which case, why didn't he damned well tell her? At least, that way she would be able to steel her heart against the pain to come. Against the projected and mostly hidden fear that, this time, his affair might be serious.

But then Natasha felt ashamed at her self-seeking—for wasn't there another part of Raffaele's life which threatened to mar its near perfection? His beautiful half sister, who was nearly a whole generation younger than him. Could that be the reason behind his unscheduled trip to Italy?

She cleared her throat. 'Elisabetta's okay, isn't she?'

Raffaele stilled, the coffee cup almost to his lips. He put it down with a clatter, untasted. 'What makes you ask about my sister?' he questioned, in a voice of dangerous stealth.

She could hardly say *Because, in your charm-filled life, she seems to be the one area which causes you concern*. That really *would* be stepping over the boundaries of acceptable behaviour. Natasha shrugged, remembering the anxious phone call he had taken from Elisabetta's psychiatrist a couple of weeks ago, which had resulted in him sitting in his study until darkness had fallen. It had been left to Natasha to wander in unnoticed and gently wonder if he wanted to put the light on, to remind him that he had a dinner engagement that evening.

'Just a hunch that all wasn't well.'

'Well, don't *have* hunches!' he flared. 'I don't pay you to have hunches!'

She stared at him, and his words felt as if

they had lanced through her heart. 'No, of course you don't. I shouldn't have said anything. I'm sorry.'

But Raffaele saw the faint tremble of her lips, which she'd tried and failed to hide, and relented with a sigh. 'No, I am the one who should be sorry, *cara*. I should not have spoken to you that way.'

But he had—and maybe he would continue to do so—and could she bear that? Natasha pinned her shoulders back as once more she felt the distant beat of apprehension—and this time it wasn't about Raffaele, but about her.

Didn't they say that familiarity bred contempt—was that why he thought he could talk to her any old way and she would just take it? Oh, yes, sometimes he called her *cara*—but that was more a term of endearment. He certainly didn't mean it in the romantic 'darling' sense.

Was she blinding herself to the fact that her position here was slowly being eroded? Was she going to wait until it became untenable before she had the courage to walk away from him?

She was beginning to recognise that as Sam grew older he would begin to notice the things which made him different from his schoolfriends. That the sumptuous home in which he lived was not really *his* home, but belonged to his mother's billionaire employer. How long before that started to matter and his friends started making fun of him for being different?

'I'd better go and get on,' she said stiffly. 'I want to make a cake—Sam's bringing a friend home for tea.' And she turned away before he could see the stupid tears which were threatening to prick at the corners of her eyes.

But Raffaele saw the rigid set of her shoulders and, for once, he realised he had hurt her. He knew that whatever else happened, Natasha didn't deserve that. Maybe it was time that he told someone other than his attorney. Troy saw things only in black-and-white, in the way that lawyers did. That was what they were paid to do—to deal with practicalities, not emotion.

But, even for a man who had spent his life running from emotion and all its messy consequences, sometimes, like now, facing it seemed unavoidable. And Natasha was a woman—they seemed to do emotion better than men. Certainly, better than this man. Wouldn't a feminine perspective from an impartial party be useful? What possible harm could there be to run it past her?

Maybe it was true what they said—that if

you spoke the words out loud it made you see them differently.

Raffaele had spent most of his thirty-four years pressing all the right buttons and had achieved huge international success, but what he liked best was the control that success gave him and the power which came with it. But these past weeks he had felt it slipping away from him—and the sensation made him uneasy.

'Natasha?'

'What?' she answered, but she didn't turn back; she was too busy blinking away the last of her tears.

Natasha would tell him the truth, even if he didn't want to hear it. 'Elisabetta's in a clinic,' he said bluntly. 'She has been secretly flown to England, and I'm terrified the press are going to find her.'

# CHAPTER TWO

NATASHA froze, her own fears crumbling to unimportant dust as she tried to take in what Raffaele had just told her—a lightning bolt from the blue. *'What?'*

'My sister has been admitted to a private clinic in the south of England, with an acute anxiety attack,' Raffaele said, as if he were reading from a charge sheet.

Natasha blinked away her thoughtlessly self-indulgent tears and turned round to face him, her hands automatically reaching out towards him in an instinctive gesture of comfort. But she saw him flinch and stare at them as if they were something untoward—which she guessed they were—and they dropped to her sides like stones.

'We've been trying to keep it out of the papers,' he said, still in that same, flat voice.

'We?'

'Me. Troy. The doctors in charge. They're

worried that it will add to her stress. If the papers get hold of it, then she'll be harassed when they discharge her—and it'll drag her right back down. The security at the clinic is tight, but there are always photographers loitering around in the hope of sniffing out a new story. And you know how everyone loves this particular modern fairytale—"the girl who has everything suddenly fighting for her sanity".'

'Oh, Raffaele,' she breathed, her blue eyes growing worried as she heard the cynicism which made his voice sound so harsh. 'Poor Elisabetta! What's happened?'

He tried to make sense of it. He wanted to tell Natasha not to look at him like that, or to say his name in that sweet, soft way, that her sympathy was making him feel all kinds of stuff that he didn't need to feel right now. Like he wanted to go straight into her arms and put his head against her pure pale skin and just *hold* her. But he shook the thought away with a corresponding shake of his head.

He was supposed to be taking control—not sleepwalking into disaster by looking vulnerable in front of his damned housekeeper! He forced his mind back to the unpalatable facts.

'You know that she never had a particularly

stable upbringing,' he said, swallowing down the bitter taste in his mouth. 'She was born when my mother was trying desperately hard to please her new husband. She knew that he wanted a child—and even though she was in her early forties by then she moved heaven and earth to get pregnant.' Raffaele had been a teenager at the time, and he remembered feeling pushed aside by his mother's new obsession. But he had been protective of the baby girl when she'd arrived—though, shortly after that, he had been relieved to leave for university.

His eyes narrowed as he remembered. 'Elisabetta once told me that they were disappointed she wasn't a boy. Her father wanted someone to take over the business, and this artistic, fey girl was the antithesis of what he'd needed. Maybe that attitude sowed the seeds for her anxiety—or maybe it would have happened anyway.' He shrugged, and his face darkened— for analysis was not in his nature unless it concerned a column full of figures. 'Who knows what caused it? All I know is that it exists.'

'But has something happened?' Natasha questioned quietly. 'To bring matters to a head?'

Raffaele's black eyes pierced through her like dark lasers. 'How did you guess?'

Because that was the way of the world, thought Natasha. 'Was it a man?'

'How perceptive of you, Tasha,' he said softly, and then his mouth hardened. That wasn't the word *she* would use to describe him. 'A relationship,' he corrected acidly. 'Someone Elisabetta thought had fallen in love with her—but, of course, it was her enormous wealth which had seduced him. *Damn* the money!' he exclaimed bitterly. '*Damn* it!'

Natasha bit her lip. Sometimes working for a man as powerful as Raffaele meant telling him things that they didn't really want to hear—because no one else dared to. Except maybe for Troy, Raffaele's lawyer. He never shied away from the facts.

'That isn't really fair, is it, Raffaele? I mean, you're enormously wealthy and it doesn't impact negatively on your life, does it? You *enjoy* your money,' she pointed out, softening the home-truth with a smile. 'So you can't always say that money is the root of all evil.'

Raffaele's mouth tightened. So this was what happened when you took someone like her into your confidence! His simmering rage was directed at Natasha now, his eyes sparking ebony fire. 'You think to criticise *me?*' he demanded. 'You dare to do that?'

'No,' she replied patiently, 'I'm just trying to help you see it more clearly, that's all.'

'She should not have been mixing with such low-life!' he stormed.

'She is a young woman, Raffaele. You haven't always—'

'Haven't always, what?' he prompted dangerously.

'You haven't always displayed the greatest judgement with some of your choices of women, have you?'

*'What?'*

She met the look of smouldering disbelief in his eyes without blinking, but somehow the thought of his doe-eyed half sister breaking her heart over some gold-digger gave Natasha the courage to stand up to him. 'I draw your attention to the woman you're currently suing.'

*'Madonna mia!'* he exclaimed. 'I met her twice—and there was no intimacy. Am I to be held responsible for some lying actress who wants to use my money and my reputation to boost her career? And Elisabetta is my *sister*,' he continued stubbornly. 'It is different.'

Natasha sighed. It was that age-old double

standard again, which some men—particularly the old-fashioned macho breed, like Raffaele—applied to all women. That there were two types. Madonna and whore. She bit her lip. Which category would *she* fall into?

Her behaviour since she'd first entered the de Feretti household had been beyond reproach—but she was still a single mother, wasn't she? And, surely, that would score negatively when measured by Raffaele's exacting standards?

'Why don't you tell me what's happened?' she said softly.

He shrugged his shoulders restlessly. Her voice was cajoling—it was like the warmth of the sun on a summer's day—but, instinctively, he fought against its comfort. 'What's to tell? This *scum* bled her bank account until her attention was drawn to it—and then he ran.' His face darkened. 'But not before he had convinced her that she loved him and that she could love no other as much as him. She stopped eating. She stopped sleeping. Her skin is like paper and her arms—they are like *this*…' He joined his forefinger and thumb together in a circle to illustrate Elisabetta's emaciated limb, and another wave of pain etched its way across his features. 'She's sick, Tasha.'

His eyes narrowed as he saw the look of concern on her face. Thank God, this was only Natasha he was talking to, came one sane, fleeting thought. Nobody had ever seen Raffaele de Feretti even close to vulnerable before—and, surely, this came close. At least, Tasha didn't count.

'Are you all right?' asked Natasha anxiously.

The image of Elisabetta came floating into his mind—with her huge eyes and the waterfall of black hair which fell in a heavy curtain to her waist. Clenching his fists together, he thought how much he would like to be able to protect his vulnerable half sister from the knocks that life had waiting in store. 'I should have been able to protect her!'

Natasha opened her mouth to say that modern women were strong enough not to need protectors— but that wasn't really true, was it? Hadn't Raffaele done just that with her? Brought her in from the cold. And hadn't he treated her son as…well, if not as his own, then certainly as some distant and fondly regarded relative?

Had she forgotten how despairing she had been when she had thrown herself onto him for mercy?

She had rung his bell one night in answer to an advertisement in the newspaper for a housekeeper, and he had opened the door himself. Some time in the hours between Natasha deciding that there was no way she could carry on living in a damp house and working like a slave, the heavens had opened and she had been soaked to the skin.

'Yes?' Raffaele had demanded, 'What is it?'

Natasha had barely noticed the autocratic and irritated note in his voice—or that his black eyes had narrowed to something approaching astonishment as he took in the sodden mess she must have made.

'I've come about the job,' she'd said.

'You're too late.'

Her face'd crumpled. 'You mean, it's taken?'

He'd shaken his head impatiently. 'I mean, that you're too late. Literally. I'm not interviewing any more today. See the agency and I'll try to fit you in tomorrow.'

But Natasha was desperate—and desperation could make you do funny things. It could fire you up with a determination you didn't know you had until your back was against the wall. Particularly, if you were looking out for someone else.

'No,' she said firmly, and rushed on as she saw his expression of incredulity—because it was now or never.

'No?' he demanded. She dared to say no? To *him*?

She took a deep breath. 'If I go away now, then you might appoint someone else before me, and no one will do the job as well as me. I can promise you that, Mr de Feretti.'

'*Signor* de Feretti,' he'd corrected flintily, but his interest had been awakened by her passion and determination and by the cold light of fear which lay at the back of her eyes.

He'd opened the door a fraction wider, so that a shaft of light had illuminated her, and Raffaele'd found himself thinking that she certainly wouldn't provide much in the way of temptation—and maybe that was a good thing. Some of the younger applicants he'd seen that day had been pretty *conturbante*— sexy—and had made it clear that working for a single and very eligible bachelor was at the top of their wish-list for very obvious reasons. And the ones who'd been older had seemed itching to mother him. 'So what makes you think you'd do the job better than anyone else?' he'd demanded.

There was no possible answer to give other than the unvarnished truth, and Natasha had heard her voice wobble as she told him.

'Because no one wants the job as much as I do. No one *needs* it as much as I do, either.'

He had seen she'd been shivering. Her teeth had been chattering and her eyes had a kind of wildness about them. He thought at the time that he might be offering house-room to someone who was very slightly unhinged, but sometimes Raffaele allowed himself to be swept along by a gut feeling that was stronger than logic or reason, and that had been one of those times.

'You'd better come in,' he'd said.

'No! Wait!'

He frowned, scarcely able to believe his ears. 'Wait?'

'Can you give me a few minutes and I'll be back?'

As Raffaele'd nodded his terse agreement he'd told himself he was being a fool—and he didn't even have the fool's usual excuse of having been blinded by a beautiful face and body. She was probably the head of some urban gang—the innocent-looking stool-pigeon who had arrived ahead of her accomplices who were even now bearing down on him.

But Raffaele was strong and fit and, deep down, he didn't really think the woman was any such thing. Why, she was little more than a girl and her desperation sounded real enough, rather than the rehearsed emotion of some scam.

He'd tossed another log on the fire, which was blazing in his study, and poured himself a glass of rich, red wine. He'd almost given up on her coming back and thought that it was probably all for the best—though, his curiosity had somehow been whetted.

And then came the ringing on the door—only, this time it was even more insistent. His temper had threatened to fray as he'd wrenched it open.

'You are not showing a very good example in interview technique!' he'd grated, and then had seen that the woman was carrying a bundle—evident, even to his untutored eyes, as being a sleeping child—and there'd been a buggy on his front step. 'What the *hell* is this?'

Without thinking, he'd pulled her inside out of the howling storm, swearing softly in Italian as he'd directed her in towards the fire, where she sank to her knees in front of the leaping flames, the child still in her arms, and let out a low, crooning sound of relief.

'My friend's been looking after my b-baby in the bus shelter while I came to see you.'

For a moment, he'd felt fury and pity in

equal measures—but something else, too. He would help her, yes—but only if she proved she was worth helping. And, unless this mystery woman dried her eyes and pulled herself together, he would kick her back out on the street, where she belonged.

'Hysterics won't work in this case,' he'd said coldly. 'Not with me.'

Just in time, Natasha had recognised that he'd meant it and, sucking in a shuddering breath, she'd looked down at Sam. How did he manage to still be asleep? she'd asked herself with something close to wonder.

'How old is he?' Raffaele'd asked.

She'd lifted her face to his. It glowed in the firelight and had been wet with rain and tears, and he'd suddenly found himself thinking that her eyes were exceptionally fine—pale, like a summer sky.

'How on earth d-did you know he was a boy?' she'd questioned shakily.

He'd heard the strong and fierce note of maternal pride and, unexpectedly, he'd smiled. 'He's dressed entirely in blue,' he'd said, almost gently.

Natasha had looked down and, sure enough, the hooded all-in-one and baby mitts had all been in variations on that shade. 'Oh, yes!' And, for the first time in a long, long time, she'd quivered him a smile. 'He's nearly eighteen months,' she'd added.

Raffaele had hid the sinking feeling in his heart. *Porca miseria!* What he knew about children and babies could be written on his fingernail, but even he knew that children around that age were nothing but trouble.

'But he's really good,' Natasha'd said.

It was perhaps unfortunate that Sam had chosen that precise moment to wake up. He'd taken one look at Raffaele and burst into an ear-splitting howl of rage.

There'd been a pause.

'So I see,' Raffaele'd said wryly.

'Oh, he's just tired,' Natasha'd babbled, clamping him tightly to her chest and rocking him like a little boat. 'And hungry. He'll be fine tomorrow.'

He'd noticed her assumption that they would still be around the next day, but didn't remark on it. 'Why are you in this situation? Where have you been living?'

'I've been working in a house—only, they keep asking me to do more and more, so that I hardly get a minute with Sam. And the house is damp, too—he's only just finished a cold, and I'm terrified he's going to get another. It's not somewhere I want to bring a child up.'

His eyes had narrowed. 'And what about his father? Is he going to turn up and want to stay the night with you here?'

'We don't see him,' Natasha'd said, with an air of finality.

'There isn't going to be a scene? Angry doorstep rows at midnight?'

She shook her head. 'No way.'

Raffaele'd looked curiously at the boy, who had been attempting to burrow into her shoulder, his thumb wobbling towards his mouth. He'd frowned. 'Where's he going to sleep?'

And with those words she'd known that she was in with a chance. That she'd had one foot in Mr—or rather—*Signor* de Feretti's expensive door and she had to prove to this rugged, but rather cold-eyed, foreigner that she deserved to stay. *They* deserved to stay.

The child had spent his first night under the Italian's roof in the same bed as his mother and when, the next morning, Raffaele'd caught Natasha trawling through the second-hand column of the local paper he'd overrode all her objections—which admittedly weren't very strong when it came to her beloved boy—to order a top-of-the-range bed which was fashioned out of wood to look like a pirate ship.

And there mother and son had been ever since.

It suited all parties very well. Raffaele knew that it was far better his big house be lived in—especially as he was away a lot, not just in the States, but Europe, too, for the de Feretti empire spread far and wide. Once, Natasha had plucked up the courage to ask him why he bothered keeping on a house in England when presumably a hotel might have been more convenient.

But he had shaken his jet-dark head. 'Because I hate them,' he'd told her, with a surprising vehemence. Hadn't he been in enough of them as a boy, following the death of his father, when he had been trailed from pillar to post by a mother determined to find herself a new rich husband? 'Hotels have no soul. All the furniture is used by faceless hundreds. The pillows slept on by others and the mattresses made love on by countless couples. Yet, when you buy stuff of your own and put it down somewhere at least you can make any house a home.'

If she hadn't been so busy trying not to bite her lip with embarrassment when he'd said that bit about making love then she might have disagreed with him—telling him that a home consisted of more than just furniture and belongings. It had to do with making it the place you most wanted to be at the end of the day. And, anyway, who was Natasha to disagree with him, when he had provided the only real home she and Sam had ever known?

When Sam had been old enough Raffaele had insisted on enrolling him to attend the nursery section of the highly acclaimed international school which was situated nearby.

'Why not?' he had queried, rather arrogantly, when she'd shaken her head.

'It's much too expensive,' Natasha'd said defensively. 'I can't afford it.'

His voice had gentled in a the way it rarely did, but which was impossible to resist when he turned it on. 'I know that. I wasn't expecting you to pay. I will.'

'I couldn't possibly accept that,' Natasha'd said, feeling as if she ought to refuse his generous offer even though her maternal heart leapt at the thought of Sam being given such a head start in life.

'You can, and you will. It makes perfect sense,' he'd drawled. 'All the other schools are far enough away to eat into your time when you take him there, and ultimately *my* time. Listen, Natasha, why don't you look at it as one of the perks of the job—rather than me giving you the use of a car, which so far you have refused to drive in London?'

Put like that, she'd found she could accept his offer gratefully, and she would never forget her joy, when Sam spoke his first few words in French and then Italian. After that Raffaele had taken to always speaking to the boy in his native tongue, and while Natasha had revelled with dazed pleasure at this evidence of her son the linguist, there had been a tiny part of her which had felt shut out. It had been enough to make her start taking Italian lessons, herself, though she kept quiet about it—in case it looked as if she was *expecting* something.

It hadn't all been plain sailing, of course. There had been the time when Sam had fallen over the step into the back garden and sustained a nasty bump to his forehead. Natasha had rushed him to the emergency room and though Raffaele had been out of the country at the time, he had listened grimly on the other end of the line as she recounted how a social worker had been round the next day to check everything out.

'Well, you should have damned well been watching him!' he had flared.

It had been unjust and unfair, but Natasha had been too eaten up with guilt to tell him that her back had been turned for just a few seconds.

And the time when Sam had found a handbag belonging to one of Raffaele's girl-friends and had decided to reinvent himself as his favourite character, Corky the Clown.

'But that's my best lipstick!' the girlfriend had screeched, as she'd dodged Sam's pink-glossed and podgy hand as he attempted to hand the decimated piece of make-up back to her.

Raffaele had laughed. 'I'll buy you another.'

The woman had pouted. 'You can't buy them over here—they're exclusive to America!' she spat. 'What a horrible little *brat!*'

And Raffaele had looked at her and known that no amount of fantastic sex was worth having to look at a nasty, spiteful face which could make a little boy cry. 'Tell you what,' he said coldly, 'I'll buy you a one-way air-ticket and you can go and get yourself a replacement.'

The girlfriend had flounced out, and Raffaele had told Natasha to make sure she kept her off-spring under control next time. But that weekend he had purchased a huge, floppy clown for Sam as a kind of silent thank-you for doing him a favour he hadn't realised he was in need of.

Of course, he never enquired about Sam's father—it was none of his business, and he didn't want to get involved in the bitter stuff which came after a couple split up.

Besides, he never really thought of Natasha in those terms. She was Sam's mother and his housekeeper, and it seemed to suit them all….

*'Dio!'* he swore. What the hell was he doing, thinking about the past, when he had the biggest problem of his life on his hands right *now*—in the present? 'What on earth am I going to do about Elisabetta, Natasha?' he demanded.

'You're doing everything you can,' she soothed. 'Presumably, she's in the best clinic that money can buy. You can support her by visiting her—'

'She isn't allowed visitors for the first four weeks,' he said flatly. 'It's one of the rules.'

Natasha nodded. How would he find that? she wondered. He, who had made up his own rules in life as he went along. 'Well, the other stuff, then. You know. Like keeping her safe.' Her eyes shone. 'You're good at that.'

But he barely heard a word she was saying, because the sudden shrill ring of the doorbell pealed out with its own particular sense of urgency.

He strode off to answer it, checking first in the peephole that it wasn't the dreaded press-pack. But it was Troy standing on the doorstep, and when Raffaele opened the door and the other man stepped inside the lawyer's grim face confirmed his worst fears.

'What is it?' he demanded. 'What's happened?'

There was a pause. 'The press have got hold of the story,' Troy said. 'They've found out where Elisabetta is.'

# CHAPTER THREE

'ARE you certain—absolutely certain?' demanded Raffaele, feeling an overwhelming sense of rage run through him at the thought of his vulnerable little sister being at the mercy of the unscrupulous press hounds. Had Elisabetta really had her cover blown? His black eyes bore into his lawyer. 'They've found out where she is?'

Troy nodded. 'I'm afraid so. I've just had a telephone call from one of our people. They're outside the clinic now,' he said.

Raffaele swore very softly and very quietly in the Sicilian dialect he had picked up one long, hot summer on the island, when he'd still been railing against the intrusion of his new stepfather. Few people could understand the language, but it had remained with him in times of anger ever since. But he recognised now that his fury was a nothing but redundant luxury and would not help solve the problem. Every problem had a solution—he knew that. Hadn't he demonstrated it over the years, time and time again?

He thought quickly. 'Come through to my study,' he said, and then glanced at Natasha, who was standing there, looking as if she wanted to say something. He waved his hand at her impatiently. 'Can you bring some coffee for Troy, Natasha? Have you eaten? I'm sure Natasha can make you something if you want.'

Troy shook his head. 'No. Coffee will be fine. And maybe one of those biscuit things, if you have them?'

'Yes, of course,' said Natasha, nodding with a brisk smile and turning away, telling herself that *of course* Raffaele was going to dismiss her like that—because what was happening with Elisabetta was *nothing whatsoever to do with her.*

She was an employee, for heaven's sake, not Raffaele's confidante—no matter how much she longed to be. And that was one of the drawbacks to the strange position she had in his life—she was part of it and, yet, nothing to do with it. Always hovering on the outskirts of it, like a tiny satellite star which relied on the mighty light of a huge planet, so that sometimes she felt she was consumed by him. But at times like this he would send her away to provide refreshments, just like the servant she really was.

After she'd gone, the two men walked through the long, arched hallway which led to his study, where they sat on either side of the desk.

'Can we kill the story?' Raffaele asked.

'Only temporarily. The *London News* is threatening to run a piece in its gossip column tonight.'

'Then slam out an injunction!'

'I already have done,' said Troy. 'But the trouble is that they aren't actually breaking any privacy code. It's just a general piece, with a few old photos, about concerns for "party-loving heiress, Elisabetta de Feretti".'

'But this is intolerable!' gritted Raffaele from between clenched teeth. 'Doesn't anyone give a damn about her well-being?'

'Not if it sells more newspapers.'

Raffaele shook his dark head, his frustration accentuated by real concern. Had he failed his sister? Been too enmeshed in the world of business to notice that her life was disintegrating around her? 'How the hell did they find out about it? Didn't the clinic give me a thousand assurances that Elisabetta's anonymity would be protected? Do we know the source of the story?'

'We do now. It's a member of staff, I'm

afraid,' said Troy slowly, sitting back in his chair as if putting distance between himself and the outburst about to follow.

For a moment Raffaele's long olive fingers curved, so that they resembled the deadly talons of some bird of prey. *'Madonna mia!'* he said, with soft venom resonating like liquid poison from his voice. 'Do you know what we shall do, Troy? We shall hunt down and find the cheating Judas who betrayed my sister. And, much as I should like to inflict a Sicilian form of punishment that they will never forget, we will discipline them formally.' He punched his fist over his heart. 'And make sure that he or she never works in a position of trust or authority again!'

There was a pause. 'You *can* do that,' said Troy, with the smooth diplomacy of his profession. 'But it will be a waste of your time and ultimately of your resources—and at a time when you can least afford to squander them.'

'You are saying that this kind of behaviour should go unpunished?' Raffaele demanded icily. 'Is that the course of action you are recommending to me?'

Troy held his hands up in a don't-shoot-the-messenger pose. 'Of course I can see that to carry out such a threat would give you satisfaction—but it would be a short-lived achievement and it would detract from your real aim of making sure that Elisabetta gets the treatment she needs without anything making it more difficult for her. And, unfortunately, all the railing and lawsuits in the world won't change human nature or the lure of big money—haven't you said that yourself, Raffaele, more times than you can count?'

Raffaele was silent for a moment while he digested the other man's words. He had known and admired Troy since both men had met at the Sorbonne in the concluding year of their international law degrees—and he had discovered Troy was that rare thing, an Englishman who spoke several languages. They had been educated as equals, had good-naturedly fought over women, and Troy had never been cowed by the black-eyed Italian who was held in so much awe wherever he went because of his presence and his unforgettable good-looks.

The fact that the Englishman had also been considered to be a bit of a sex god by the women of Paris had meant that there was no rivalry between the two men.

As well as Troy's fluency in both Italian and French, he possessed the valuable impartiality which was so much a characteristic of his nationality, and all these factors had made him the perfect choice to be personal advocate for the powerful Raffaele de Feretti. There were not many men to whom Raffaele listened, but this was one of them—and he was listening now.

'*Si,* Troy, *mio amico*—you are right, of course,' Raffaele said heavily, still feeling that he had somehow failed his sister—even though logic told him otherwise. 'So, what do we do?'

Troy placed the tips of his fingers together in an almost prayerlike gesture of careful thought. 'We run a spoiler. We take attention *away* from Elisabetta by giving them a bigger story.'

Raffaele gave a sceptical laugh. 'And how do you propose doing that?'

Troy leaned forward. 'Elisabetta is newsworthy because, yes, she's young, and beautiful, very rich and occasionally flawed—but ultimately she's famous for being your sister.'

'I think that you overestimate my interest value,' demurred Raffaele—because he had sought no publicity for himself.

Troy gave a short laugh. 'It's true that in terms of your power and your money everything that can possibly have been written on the subject already has been. But don't forget,

Raffaele, that there is one area of a your life which has held a particular fascination for the press ever since you passed puberty.'

Raffaele stared at him, his black eyes narrowing. 'Be a little more *specific,* Troy,' he instructed softly.

'They've been trying to marry you off for years!'

'So?'

'So the only story which could draw interest away from Elisabetta would be if you finally did it.'

'Did *what,* precisely?'

'Got yourself a wife,' said Troy, just as there was a rap on the door and it began to open. 'Maybe it's time you married, Raffaele!'

Natasha entered the room just in time to hear Troy's enthusiastic statement and, for a moment, she honestly thought that she might drop her tray. She felt the blood drain from her face and her knees grow weak and some terrible roaring sound deafened her ears—like the sound of an express train racing through her head.

'Natasha?' Raffaele was frowning at her. 'Are you sick?'

'I…'

'Put the damned tray down,' he instructed

tersely, but he had risen from his chair and was taking it from her himself. He put it down on the desk and caught her by the arm. 'What the hell is the matter with you?'

But with a few deep breaths Natasha had quickly recovered her equilibrium and she shook him off, telling herself that it was very important she didn't make a fool of herself.

Raffaele had been nothing but decent and fair to her over the years, and he had done more for Sam than could reasonably be expected of a boss. So she was not going to blow the whole thing by showing her distress at what was, after all, a long overdue piece of news. Or had she really expected a man like Raffaele to remain single for the rest of his life, just so that she could maintain her little fantasies about him?

'You're getting married?' she exclaimed brightly, and then forced the next word out, even though it felt like a fishbone stuck in her throat. 'Congratulations!'

Raffaele was staring at her as if she had taken leave of her senses. 'So this is how gossip begins!' he objected moodily. 'Something half overheard and then, before you know it, you are dealing with "fact"—only, it isn't fact at all. Just some crazy conjecture!'

'You mean, you're *not* getting married?' questioned Natasha cautiously, unable to prevent the wild leap of her heart, and thankful that he wouldn't be able to detect it.

'Of course I'm not getting married!' he retorted.

'I'm trying to persuade him to get married,' said Troy.

'Oh.' Natasha forced a smile as she looked at Troy, hating—just *hating*—Raffaele's smart-aleck lawyer at that moment. She cleared her throat as she began to pour their coffee. 'Isn't marriage an honourable institution that isn't supposed to be entered into lightly?' she asked, as casually as if she was enquiring whether they wanted milk or sugar. 'Who's the lucky woman?'

'I'm not talking about a *real* marriage,' said Troy. 'I'm talking about a pretend one.'

'A pretend one?' said Raffaele and Natasha at exactly the same moment, and Natasha began to fiddle around unnecessarily with the sugar bowl.

Troy nodded. 'You don't have to actually go through with it—just make the gestures. You know—you buy a whopping engagement ring and then you pose with your fiancée for the papers and she gives them a few interviews telling them where the wedding will be, where she's going to buy her dress. They love all that kind of stuff.'

'You seem remarkably well informed on the subject,' remarked Raffaele, with a sardonic elevation of his black brows.

'I try,' said Troy modestly.

'And even if I *were* to entertain such a bizarre remedy, aren't you forgetting one thing?'

'Like what?'

Raffaele's black eyes were like hard, cold jet. 'That there isn't a candidate.'

Did he hear Natasha's pent-up sigh of relief? Was that why he turned his head and fixed her with an impenetrable stare. 'Didn't you say you had a cake to make?'

Natasha blinked. Of all the times to prove that he had actually been listening to something she had to say he had to choose *this* one! 'Er…yes.'

'Well, then, run along, *cara,*' he said softly.

'Right.' Reluctantly, Natasha headed for the door, while they just carried on with their conversation as if she was invisible. Which I might as well be, she thought furiously.

'You just need someone who is prepared to go along with it,' Troy was saying.

'Like who? Oh, I can see your reasoning. It's a good idea, Troy—but there's just one problem, and it's the nightmare scenario.' Raffaele's eyes narrowed thoughtfully. 'Most women I know would be only to happy to go through with it—the difficulty would be getting them off my back afterwards.'

Troy laughed. 'Which is why we choose someone who wouldn't dare try to hang around.'

'Again, I say—*who?*'

Fascinating as she found the subject, Natasha knew that she really couldn't justify hanging around any longer, and she was almost out of the door when her eagle eye spotted a rogue little yellow plastic brick lying underneath one of the two wing chairs by the bookcase.

Now, how the hell had that gotten in here—especially when Sam wasn't even supposed to go into Raffaele's study? She was so fastidious about keeping all signs of young children carefully hidden away. Raffaele might be tolerant, and kinder to her son than his position warranted, but he certainly didn't want to be tripping up over model soldiers every time he came home.

She made a little exclamation of annoyance as she leaned over to retrieve the brick, and as the sound diverted his attention Raffaele found his eyes drawn to her bent figure.

Nobody could accuse Natasha of vanity—

indeed, the garments she wore for work wouldn't have been out of place in a boot-camp and they'd never have been Raffaele's choice for a woman—never in a million years. He'd often used to think that here was a woman who would never distract him as she went about her work.

Maybe it was something to do with the fact that his nerves were on edge, or that it had been a long time since he'd had someone in his bed. Or maybe it was just something as simple as the fact that the moment had caught her with the material of her dress stretched tight across her derrière. Raffaele swallowed. And a very attractive derrière it was, too.

He narrowed his eyes and became aware of Troy's gaze following exactly the same path as his.

'Oh, yes,' said Troy softly. '*Yes*. That is *perfect*.'

Why was it that Raffaele found himself looking at his lawyer with cold distaste, wanting to tell him not to *dare* look at Natasha in that way—that she deserved his respect, not his predatory gaze? He shook himself. Predatory? Over *Natasha?*

She was straightening up now, with a piece of yellow plastic held between her fingers, and the fabric fell loose away from where it had been moulded to the tight, high curve of her buttocks. And all Raffaele could think was *why the hell had he never noticed that before?*

'You wouldn't have wanted to have stepped on *that* with bare feet!' she said triumphantly, and put it in her pocket as she marched out without a backwards glance.

Raffaele watched as she shut the door behind her, and suddenly there was Troy, sitting with some dumb, expectant grin on his face, looking at him as if he had found the key to the universe.

'Well? What do you think, Raffaele? Isn't this the answer to our predicament? Wouldn't *Natasha* do?'

# CHAPTER FOUR

'No!' Raffaele snapped back, in an icy voice. 'Natasha would *not* do! She's my housekeeper, for *Dio's* sake!'

Outside the study door, the sound of her name halted Natasha right in her tracks and presented her with an age-old moral dilemma. Should she stay or should she go? Should she listen or not? But, surely, if they were talking about *her* didn't she have every *right* to listen?

Heart thumping, and with misgivings which were making her forehead ice into a cold sweat, she put her head close to the door. Their voices were muffled, but she could make out certain words like *unsuitable, inappropriate.* And then something else, which ended with Raffaele saying, quite loudly and quite forcefully, 'No one would ever believe it!'

And Troy's response. 'Why not ask her?'

She heard the sound of a chair being scraped

back, and instinct made her move quickly away from her giveaway position. She hurried down to the kitchen, realising that time was tight if she wanted to have the cake made before she went out to collect Sam.

The radio was blaring as she changed her mind about lemon drizzle and instead made cupcakes, which she iced in lurid shades of green and blue, especially designed to appeal to small boys—and to hell with the additives!

Despite the apron she'd put on, she'd still managed to get splodges of cake mixture over her dress—and she was going to have to leave in a minute. She ran upstairs and changed into something warmer—because the autumn afternoons were beginning to bite.

She put on a pale blue sweater, which brought out the colour in her eyes, and a pair of old jeans Then she brushed her hair and wove it into its habitual French plait. Her fingers hesitated over the little tub of lipgloss which had been on special offer at the chemist back in the summer, and which some impulse had made her buy. She'd only used it a couple of times, and it didn't really seem to be *her,* so she'd put the top back on and had never used it again.

So what was it that made her pick it up today?

Did it have something to do with the way the two men had looked at her in the study—or rather the way they'd *not* looked at her? As if she was some old piece of furniture—reliably comfortable, but not something you'd want to show off to a guest.

Defiantly, she opened it and stroked on some of the strawberry-scented gloss. Perhaps some of her reluctance to dress up had come from knowing that she could never compete with the other mothers, who arrived at the school looking as if they'd stepped out of the pages of a glossy magazine. Maybe that was why she was always being mistaken for one of the nannies—though she had to admit that most of *them* made more of an effort than she did.

Outside, the late-afternoon sky was a clear blue and the trees were etched against it in startling relief. All the leaves were turning rich shades of bronze and toffee and gold and, in the distance, she thought she could smell the faint drift of smoke, which was unusual in London, though this area was exclusive enough to have gardens big enough to cope with bonfires.

Natasha was suddenly overcome with the sense of nostalgia which autumn always provoked. The end of the summer and the start of winter and soon Sam beginning full-time school. During no other season was she quite so aware of the passing of time as this, when the leaves began their dizzy spiralling dance to the ground below.

There were luxury cars in abundance parked in the streets near the school—most people had to travel from all over the capital to get there—and Natasha never forgot to count her blessings that she lived close enough to walk there.

She watched as the children began to file out in their rather old-fashioned uniform of knee-length shorts for the little boys and kilts for the girls, along with thick sweaters which looked like home-knits, and sturdy shoes and dark socks. Sam was excitedly anticipating the time when he would graduate to long trousers—like the 'big' boys at the middle school—and Natasha began to wonder how long she could let things continue like this. With Sam getting more and more used to the luxurious lifestyle which Raffaele could afford to give him. Was it time for her to start getting real? To live within *her* means?

'*Maman!*' Sam called as he came running over, his little friend in tow. 'You're wearing lipstick!'

'Hello, darling—was it a French day today?'

'You're wearing lipstick!' accused her son again.

'Yes, I am—do you like it?' She smiled down at Sam's best friend. 'Hello, Serge. How are you?'

*'Très bien, merci!'* replied Serge, with the solemn confidence learnt from his French diplomat father.

'Well, that's good,' she replied, as the three of them began to walk the route home, which took them past the area's best conker tree. 'I've made monster cakes!'

'Monster cakes?' Serge frowned as Sam began to scoop up the shiny brown nuts. 'But what are monster cakes?'

'It means you turn into a monster if you eat them!' chanted Sam. 'Will Raffaele be there?'

'He's probably busy, darling—we'll see.'

*'Oh!'*

The boys played with their conkers in the garden and then came inside for supper. Because it was Friday, there was no homework, so she left them playing a complicated game with battleships. She was just wondering whether Raffaele wanted her to make him supper when she almost collided with him.

'Just the person I wanted to see,' he said grimly.

It didn't sound that way. And why was he

looking at her like that, with an expression on his face she had never seen before? The black eyes were brilliant and piercing and they narrowed as they swept over her, as if they were assessing her for something—but what?

Some kind of sixth sense set off a distant clamour which seemed to make Natasha acutely aware of the pulsing of her blood—as if something had just sprung to life within her. Alarmingly, she felt the tips of her breasts begin to rub against the rough lace of her bra and the corresponding flood of colour to her cheeks.

'Well, here I am,' she said.

But Raffaele wasn't listening. He was struck by the way her cheeks were looking uncharacteristically pink—like the wild roses of summer. And by the way…the way… *Madre di Dio,* but this could not be happening!

Irresistibly, he found his gaze locked onto the luscious curve of her breasts, and he started wondering whether this was because of what had happened earlier—an awakening which had been triggered by something as simple as a woman bending down to pick up a toy. The sudden realisation that behind the guise of her unerring efficiency Natasha *was* a woman. A real flesh-and-blood one at that. He found that he wanted to cup his palms over those buttocks and bring her right up close against him.

'Any more news about Elisabetta?'

Her question was like an icy bath on his senses, and he discovered that he had been guilty of some very impure thoughts, indeed—and *that* wasn't on his agenda at all. He hardened his voice. Elisabetta was the reason he was about to do all this—and the *only* reason, he reminded himself.

'No,' he said, staring at her mouth and thinking that there was something different about *that,* too. Was it all shiny and pink? Or was that just his imagination? He frowned. Was he out of his mind to go through with this crazy scheme? And yet hadn't he been racking his brains all day and coming up with remarkably few solutions to this particular dilemma? For all his wealth and power and connections there were some things he *couldn't* control, and the press was one of them. 'Is Sam here?'

'He's downstairs with Serge. He's got a new conker he wants to show you.'

For a moment the tension on his face eased, the faint smile nudging at the corners of his mouth completely transforming his rugged features.

'I'll go down and take a look.' He raised his brows. 'And later—will he be here then?'

She shook her head and frowned. 'No, he's going to stay over at Serge's—it's his turn this week. Is there a problem?'

'Not really,' he said smoothly. 'I suggest that you and I eat together.'

Natasha shrugged. It wasn't as if their eating together was unknown. She didn't go out that often—and certainly not when Raffaele was around. She felt that being there was part of the fabulous deal he had made with her—she made the house warm and comfortable when he was home.

She wanted to ask him what was on his mind and, yet, there was something very censorious in his eyes which dared her to even try—a dark, warning light that made her very aware of his position over her. Because—despite all their familiarity and the usual ease with which they lived their lives—sometimes Raffaele unmistakably pulled rank, and he was doing it now. This wasn't a casual suggestion that they might eat supper together, it was an order, and Natasha's pulse began to race. 'Sure. Would you like me to cook something special?'

'No. That won't be necessary. I'll cook.'

Raffaele? *Cook?* 'R-right.'

Her anxiety grew as she saw the boys off

when Serge's impossibly glamorous nanny came to collect them. Natasha could tell that she was dawdling unnecessarily in the hall.

'Signor de Feretti—he is at home?' the girl asked guilelessly, her enormous dark eyes like velvet saucers, searching the tempting spaces behind Natasha's shoulders.

'He is—somewhere. Quite busy, I expect—unless it was something specific?'

'I want to go to Italy to be a nanny next year—I thought maybe he could tell me some things.'

'Signor de Feretti is very busy,' said Natasha, a little more crisply than she had intended. 'Perhaps you should try one of the agencies? I'm sure they can tell you everything you need to know.'

After they'd gone, the house seemed more echoing than usual, and Natasha could hear the sounds of Raffaele clanking stuff around in the basement kitchen in between the phone ringing and ringing. He shouted up to tell her to leave it on the answer-machine, but then his mobile started, and he must have picked it up because she could hear the low, urgent sound of his voice.

She felt odd—as if she wasn't quite sure of her place anymore, as if something had changed but no one had bothered to tell her about it.

Slowly, she went downstairs, where Raffaele was stirring something in a pot. He wore jeans—old, faded and blue—hugging his lean hips and skating down the muscular shaft of his long legs. With the jeans he wore a shirt made of thick white cambric, through which she could just make out the hard outline of his torso.

He heard her come in and turned round and, inconsequentially, she noticed that there were two buttons of his shirt undone and that dark hair curled there—a shadowy dark triangle, contrasted against the snowy material. His black hair was still damp, as if he had recently showered and his feet were bare. Natasha was suddenly filled with an overwhelming wave of longing and weakness.

'Hungry?' he questioned.

She shook her head, wanting to ask him what was going on—why he was talking to her and treating her in a way which made him seem like a stranger to her.

'Not yet. I'd like a drink, please.'

He frowned. 'You mean, a *drink* drink?'

She glanced over at the already open bottle of red. 'If that's all right.'

'Sure. It's just that you don't usually—'

'Drink? No, I don't.' But Natasha had had

enough of this walking-on-eggshells feeling. If he was about to tell her he wanted to sack her, then why the hell didn't he just come out with it—instead of all this awkwardness which left her feeling lost and helpless? 'And *you* don't usually behave like this.'

'Like what?' he demanded.

'Oh, Raffaele—I don't *know!*'

He stared at her and, for a moment, he almost made a joke about the glaring lack of feminine logic, the way he might usually have done, but he poured her a glass of wine, instead, and turned the heat off from underneath the pan. Then he drank a large mouthful of his own drink and sat down on the edge of the large kitchen table, his black eyes fixed unwaveringly on her face. 'You know what Troy and I were discussing earlier?'

'You discussed rather a lot. And then I left,' she said pointedly.

He realised that there was no *correct* way of going about what he was going to propose. That maybe being businesslike was the only way in which either of them might find it acceptable.

'I have a favour to ask you, Natasha,' he said quietly.

'Go on.'

'You've heard the phone ringing? *Si?* It was the editors of two national dailies, asking about Elisabetta—wanting to know more details. For now, a blank refusal to tell them anything seems to have worked, but they won't let up—I've seen it happen before. I've spent the afternoon going over and over what might be the best course of action. I thought of taking her to the States, or back to Italy—but the former is a long way for her to travel at the moment, and, as you know, the worst place in the world for her at the moment is Italy—and that man.'

There was a pause while he looked at her—at the mediocre jeans she wore, with a very ordinary sweater. At the cheap canvas shoes on her feet—footwear which no woman of his acquaintance would ever be seen wearing. He thought about all the things Troy had said and found himself agreeing with some of them. What alternative did he have? No woman knew him the way she did—and no other woman would be prepared to take him only on *his* terms.

Would she do it? he wondered, and—more importantly—would anyone really believe that he, Raffaele de Feretti, would enter into a relationship with someone like Natasha Phillips? But his mind was made up. In a day of ever-decreasing possibilities, this remained the only one which made any sense to him.

'I want you to become engaged to me, Natasha,' he said slowly.

For a moment her mind played tricks on her as a thousand latent fantasies sprang into glorious Technicolor life. Dreams that she'd tried desperately hard not to nurture were sudenly given life—dreams about a man who had seemed way beyond the grasp of someone like her.

Yet sometimes, when the dark cloak of night banished all reasonable objections, her hopes would flare as she allowed herself to think about his glowing olive skin, with his black eyes set in it like dark jewels. Or the autocratic and proud features and the body which was all hard muscle and sinew. She would allow herself a heavenly glimpse of what it would be like to be held in his arms, to be kissed by such a mouth as Raffaele's. And then be left aching and empty when the morning light mocked her for her foolish longings.

But Raffaele was asking her…to *marry* him? If Natasha hadn't been so befuddled by events she might have made the connection with what she'd overheard earlier—as it was, she just stared at him, her lips parted.

'You want to marry me?' she questioned breathlessly.

'No. I want us to become engaged.'

The first cold drip of reality pinged into her brain. 'Why?' she asked numbly.

Why the hell did she think? 'Because it will kill the Elisabetta story stone-dead.'

Somehow Natasha kept the hurt from her face—the stupid hurt which might let him catch a glimpse of the crazy fantasies she had been nurturing. Instead, she used her matter-of-face voice—the one she sometimes used if she thought he looked tired and said so. 'You don't think that it might look like a set-up? That any editor worth their salt will realise that?'

'What they think and what they print are two different matters—and no editor will be foolish or cynical enough to come out and say that the engagement is just a—'

'Publicity stunt?' she put in shakily.

'A damage limitation exercise,' he corrected.

There was a long pause while Natasha tried to work though what the repercussions might be, but her head was whirling with it. 'And just when are you proposing that we get 'engaged'?' she asked quietly.

Raffaele relaxed by a fraction. 'We can go and

buy a ring as soon as you like.' His eyes narrowed as he saw her bite her lip and, for the first time, he began to consider how such an action might sit awkwardly with such a quiet and plain woman. 'I can understand your reservations—'

'Can you?' She gave a short laugh.

'Of course I can. It seems a little *theatrical,* but we really ought to make it look as real as possible.'

*As real as possible.* Natasha kept her face in check. Not a hint of disappointment would he read there. 'But it isn't real, is it?' she questioned, almost brightly. 'None of it.'

Raffaele laughed, some of the tension beginning to leave him as he realised that she was joking. This was going to be ridiculously easy! 'No, of course it isn't! Don't worry, Natasha— it can be the shortest engagement on record, if you like. Just long enough to take some of the heat off Elisabetta. You can even keep the ring afterwards, if you want—or sell it, of course.'

There was a dreadful kind of silence. 'That won't be necessary,' she said, in a choked kind of voice. 'I'm not asking for any kind of payment.'

He realised that he had said the wrong thing. 'I didn't mean it like that. Really, I didn't.' He stared at her, waiting for some light-hearted response and, when none came, he softened his voice in the way he only dared risk doing with her—because Natasha was sensible enough not to see anything in it other than friendly concern. 'You're the only woman I know who won't read anything else into it. It makes perfect sense, when you think about it—since we know each other so well.'

Natasha looked at him. He just didn't get it, did he? They *didn't* know each other at all. If he had known even a *fraction* about the way her mind operated, then he would know that he'd really insulted her with his crass suggestion that she keep the ring or sell it. As if such a ring wouldn't be anything other than a mocking reminder of what could have been but which never would.

His words had opened up the great, gaping chasm which lay between pointless dreams and harsh reality. She was useful to Raffaele, nothing more than that—and never more so than now.

Raffaele's eyes narrowed as another far more unsettling objection occurred to him. 'Unless you have some man-friend of your own?' he suggested silkily. 'Someone who might object on the grounds of your relationship with him?'

Had Natasha stupidly thought that her pain

threshold had been reached? Because as she shook her head in answer to his question she was discovering a capacity for more. And, oddly enough, this suggestion hurt more than anything preceding it—that he could think she might be seeing someone. *And that he shouldn't even care!* But Natasha forced herself to embrace the pain which washed over her.

Maybe this was the wake-up call she needed. The one which would banish all her wistful longings once and for all and allow her to move on with her life. To maybe start looking out for herself—even to think that one day she might meet a man she cared about enough to consider spending her life with. It was true he wouldn't be Raffaele de Feretti—but if she chose to compare other men with *him,* then she was going to end up a very bitter and lonely woman.

'What *exactly* will this so-called engagement entail?' she asked.

'We'll announce it, obviously—and then just a few high-profile occasions when we'll need to be seen at together. Nothing too onerous,' he added, with the glitter of a smile.

How *privileged* he was, she thought suddenly—and not simply in the material sense.

Here was a man who could snap his fingers and get exactly what he wanted.

'And what about Sam?' she asked, her heart undergoing a swift somersault of misgiving.

'What about him?'

'It's going to confuse him,' she said quietly.

There was silence for a moment.

'Will a five-year-old boy even notice?' he questioned. 'This isn't something that's going to make any difference at home. Nothing is going to change for Sam, is it? We can explain about Elisabetta being sick, if you want, and that us being a couple is simply to help her—as long as he doesn't tell anyone else. Or we can just answer his questions if and when they come up. All Sam needs to know is that we're still going to be friends afterwards.'

She stared into his uncomprehending eyes. Friends? Not really. *And he doesn't even realise that, either, does he? Nor does he have any inkling of how much my little boy worships him and would love more than anything for the engagement to be real. I have to leave this house and this man,* Natasha thought suddenly—*and I have to do it soon.* Perhaps this whole peculiar scheme would make it that bit easier….

'You want some time to think about it?' asked Raffaele, frowning.

'No. I've made my mind up. I'll do it.' After everything he'd done for her, it was the least she could do.

He slanted her a smile and held his glass up to chink hers in a toast. *'Stupendo!'* he said softly. He saw her lips tremble and idly wondered what it would be like to kiss them, to seal their 'engagement' in the more traditional way. He was surprised by the stir of interest he felt. But this was a game. A pretence. Nothing more. And the rather more worrying question of authenticity began to rear its head.

'You're going to have to do something about your wardrobe, of course,' he said abruptly.

Natasha nearly choked on her wine. 'What's that supposed to mean?'

The good thing about knowing someone as well as he did Natasha, was that Raffaele could tell it like it really was—and the truth was a luxury you didn't get to use with most people.

'Well, obviously, the press are going to love the rich man-poor girl aspect of the affair—the fact that you work for me—but if you look too…well, too…'

'Too, what, Raffaele?' she questioned, in a high, clear voice.

'My taste in women is well known,' he said bluntly, wondering why she hid her bottom when it happened to be such a shapely one. 'And, at the moment, you do not fulfill any of the criteria.'

There was a pause, as if he was letting the full, hurtful implication sink in.

'You will need to dress in beautiful things,' he continued. 'Tomorrow you will go and buy yourself an entire new wardrobe and charge it to my account. Buy what you like,' he added. But even thinking about her shapely curves was making made him grow hard—something which was *not* part of the deal. 'And perhaps you should do something with your hair while you're at it,' he finished.

There was a space of about ten seconds when Natasha was seriously tempted to tell him exactly what he could do with his bogus engagement and then tell him how incredibly *insulting* he had managed to be before storming off. But the possibility dissolved away— because there was no way she could follow through. How could she fail to do anything other than help Raffaele when he needed her help just as he had helped her that wet, dark night when she'd turned up on his doorstep? Doing this would make them even. Quits. And then she could leave him.

Because after this there would be nowhere to go with this relationship—and she had no right to get angry simply because Raffaele looked on her as nothing more than someone who worked for him. She did! If she had invested too much emotional energy and hopes in her boss, then she had only herself to blame.

'I haven't done anything with my hair for years.' Natasha touched her fingers to the thick French plait which hung all the way down her back. Wasn't Raffaele giving her the opportunity to do what all those TV makeover programmes aimed for—make her into the woman she'd always wanted to be?

*And what kind of woman is that?*

The sobering truth was that she didn't know.

# CHAPTER FIVE

THE NEXT day, Natasha went to the most famous department store she could think of and booked an appointment with a personal shopper.

'Call me Kirsty,' said the grinning redhead. 'And then tell me what it is you're looking for.'

Natasha drew a deep breath. She knew what Raffaele wanted—someone who looked as little like a housekeeper as possible—so why not give it to him?

'I want a complete change of image,' she said.

She noticed that Kirsty didn't contradict her. 'We can do that. And what's your budget?'

This part took a little getting used to. 'I don't actually have a budget,' admitted Natasha.

Kirsty's eyebrows underwent a rapid elevation. 'You mean, money's no object?'

'Kind of,' Natasha agreed, but some stubborn frugal ethic forced her to add, 'Of course, I don't actually want to *waste* any money.'

'There's no such thing as waste—not where clothes and beauty products are concerned,' said Kirsty smoothly. 'We women owe it to ourselves to look as good as possible. Remember that, Natasha.'

'I'll try,' said Natasha faintly.

It was not something she had ever done— blazed her way through a shop and kitted herself out from head to toe. When she'd been growing up, money had been tight, then she'd been a student and then Sam had come along. The array of goods on sale was dazzling, and Natasha was glad to have Kirsty to run an experienced eye over colour and design.

As Kirsty told her, most women didn't get to the age of twenty-five without some of idea of what colours suited them—but what most of them failed to do was to try some unusual and different shades which would not have been their first and obvious choice. She put Natasha into deep leaf-green and terracotta, deep blues and purples, as well as her more usual pastels. There were silk-satins for evening, deliciously filmy underwear and clothes that were described as 'leisurewear'.

'Now the good bit—shoes. Here, try these!' suggested Kirsty.

Natasha tottered around in front of the mirrors on a pair of impossibly high heels—which she resolutely rejected.

'But they make your legs look like stilts,' objected Kirsty.

'I'm not sure I *want* legs like stilts—and, anyway, I can't actually walk in them!'

In the end she compromised with something lower—but Kirsty insisted that if she didn't buy the sinful-looking shoes in scarlet patent she would regret it for the rest of her life. And Natasha supposed that she must have been on some kind of a high, because she found herself agreeing.

She shopped until she almost dropped, but her fatigue was quickly put to flight by a pedicure—possibly the most heavenly and restful experience of her entire life. Her feet were pummelled and scrubbed and soaked in sweet-smelling warm water, her toenails buffed and polished, so that, in the end, they didn't look or feel like Natasha's feet at all. She felt so comfortable that she allowed herself to be shown how to make her face up, and she bought the foundation, mascara, eyeshadows, blusher and lipsticks which a fancy-looking chart said were suitable for her particular colouring. Then the beautician suggested a leg and bikini wax.

'Oh, I'm not sure,' she said doubtfully, wondering when it would ever end.

'Is it a gentleman paying for all this?' asked Kirsty delicately. 'Yes? Well, then, let me assure you that a leg wax *will* be required.'

Natasha could hardly object to the insinuation—just as she could hardly tell Kirsty that sex wasn't part of the deal. Hadn't she told herself that if she was going to enter into this elaborate subterfuge then she would do it with good grace? More importantly, that she would actually try to *enjoy* herself.

'Now, you're ditching those jeans,' said Kirsty determinedly, 'and you're going to wear some of your brand-new wardrobe. The old Natasha is dead—long live the new one!'

The new Natasha was then taken to a fancy hairdresser close to South Molton Street where, magically, their most talented stylist managed to find a slot free at the end of a busy afternoon. That was money talking again, Natasha guessed.

'So, what are we looking at, dear?' he questioned, lifting long strands of hair one by one and then letting them drop down again—so that in the mirror Natasha thought she looked like a kind of octopus. 'One inch? Two?'

'Make it look fabulous,' said Natasha recklessly, because she'd bought Kirsty a champagne cocktail for helping her and had had one, herself, and had rather glowingly decided that it would be ridiculously easy to get used to having a lot of money.

'Fabulous it is!' trilled the stylist with camp excitement.

Natasha had missed out on the frivolous side of growing up. The aunt who had brought her up had been kind, but distant—and terribly old-fashioned. She had thought it demeaning for women to rely on their looks to help them get on in life. 'A woman should use her brains, not her body,' she used to tell Natasha as she pored over her schoolbooks.

Little wonder that Natasha had been ill equipped to deal with all the pitfalls of a modern world from which she had been rigorously shielded. Her arrival at university after her all-girls' school had been like being hurled down a wind tunnel—it had left her gasping and reeling. Her prim innocence had attracted a certain type of man—the kind who saw the taking of virginity as his due, but who ran a million miles when he discovered she was pregnant.

As the colourist pulled various strands of hair through an alien-looking, silver cap and the cutter snipped away, Natasha wondered whether she had just stayed stuck in a rut. She had been safely cocooned at home with her aunt, and now she was safely cocooned at Raffaele's. Her one foray into the outside world had left her feeling scorched and so she had retreated from it. Well, not so safe anymore, she thought, as the dryer whooshed the shorter, brighter strands of hair around her head.

'There!' said the stylist, beaming.

Natasha blinked, hardly recognising the face which gazed back at her from the mirror. The dress and the make-up were amazing, yes—and the lingerie she was wearing underneath made her feel completely different from the usual drab mum she considered herself to be. But it was the hair which effected the most dramatic transformation of all. No wonder thieves wore wigs to disguise themselves, she thought.

The stylist had lopped several inches off and cut into the ends of it, so that it hung in a thick, scented curtain to her shoulders. With the colourist's help it was now a mass of subtle variations, a warmer and lighter version of her original shade, so she would have described it as golden or honey instead of the ubiquitous pale mousy-brown.

'What do you think?' the stylist asked excitedly. 'There's still enough length to wear it up, if you want to.'

'It...well, it doesn't look like me,' she breathed.

'That was the idea, dear!' he commented wryly.

It had been easy during her makeover to forget just why she was doing it. But as the taxi neared the house, laden down with enough shopping bags to sink a battleship, Natasha began to feel nervous.

Would Raffaele think she'd lost it and had gone completely over the top? More importantly, could she actually go through with this whole crazy scheme?

But something had happened as she had stared at herself in the mirror in the hairdresser's. Something which she couldn't really put into words, but it had a lot to do with giving her a certain *sense* of herself—as if when she'd gazed back at that calm, perfectly made-up face she had seen someone different from the person she considered herself to be.

Not Natasha the mum.

Nor Natasha the housekeeper.

Or Natasha who knew nothing about men.

She had blinked at the very real discovery that

she could be whoever she wanted to be—she just hadn't found out who that was. Not yet.

The taxi drew up outside the imposing townhouse and the driver tooted his horn. 'Anyone inside? You'll need a crane to help you get those in,' he joked.

Raffaele appeared at the door. And stood for one long, silent moment staring down at her, black eyes narrowed and impenetrable, before he ran down the steps.

He paid the taxi and took the shopping bags from her, and Natasha was suddenly and acutely aware of his proximity, of the raw masculine heat radiating from his body and the sensual trace of lemon and sandalwood aftershave which was so particular to him. Her newfound confidence began to seep away, drained by the ebony blaze of his gaze as it raked over her. *Say something,* she pleaded silently.

The taxi roared away and they stood on the pavement—facing each other like two people who'd just met.

His eyes travelled from the tip of her expensively shorn head down to the dress of fine cashmere which moulded itself to her body in a way he'd never seen a dress do to her before. A leather belt was slung low on her hips and leather boots slouched midway down her slender legs. Raffaele was unprepared for the savage kick of lust.

'Where's S-Sam?' she questioned unsteadily.

Reluctantly, he tore his gaze away from her legs to her face—to eyes that were newly huge and the soft glimmer of rose-petal lips. 'Inside. We were watching a DVD but he's just fallen asleep—worn out from playing football. He's had a busy day.' There was a pause, and when he spoke again, it was with a soft and almost dangerous stealth. 'And so have you, *cara mia,* to judge by your appearance.'

Her heart missed a beat—for that was surely disapproval which glimmered from those coal-black eyes, a note of condemnation which had deepened his voice? 'You don't like it?'

'I didn't say that.'

'You didn't say the opposite, though, did you—that you liked it?'

His mouth pursed into the mockery of a kiss. *'Madre di Dio,'* he mused. 'Is this what a little finery does to a woman? It changes her from demure to demanding?'

'That's not fair, Raffaele!'

'Isn't it? And is it fair to dress like a siren— to say to a man you may look but not touch?'

'I didn't say that!'

'Oh, you *didn't?*' His eyes widened, like a cat's. 'That is exactly what I wanted to hear, *bella mia,*' he murmured. He dropped the bags to the pavement, pulled her into his arms, and Natasha found herself being almost lifted against the hard, muscular length of his body. With a low laugh of what sounded like triumph he raised his hand to catch hold of her beautifully cut hair, winding his fingers through its silken depths and bringing it towards him so that her gasping face was lifted to his.

'Raffaele!'

'What is it, *mia bella?*' he taunted. 'You want me to kiss you? Is that it?'

She opened her mouth to say no, but the word never came—and, if it had, it would have been a lie. Maybe he knew that—just as he seemed to know the precise moment to crush his lips down against hers in a powerful kiss that was about possession as much as passion, like a man staking his claim.

Was it because she had not been kissed by a man for so long that Natasha reacted so completely and instinctively to Raffaele's kiss—or was it simply Raffaele effect?

Whatever lay behind it, all Natasha knew was

that she seemed powerless to do anything other than close her eyes and open her lips and submit to the sweet, heady pressure. Her hands flew up to grip at his shoulders as she felt the soft graze of his teeth, the tantalising flick of his tongue against the roof of her mouth. Did he sense how helpless she felt. Or was her little cry of disbelieving pleasure a giveaway in itself?

Because hadn't Raffaele's kiss been her greatest and most forbidden wish of all—the one which had used to eat away at her when she least expected it? When he curved her that hard smile before he left in the mornings. Or when he returned from abroad and she had missed him more than he would ever know. Or occasionally—and much too dangerously—when he had just taken a shower and his black hair still glistened, and she'd imagine the hard, olive-skinned body standing beneath steaming jets of water.

Well, this kiss was real enough and, for once, reality far exceeded the kiss of her imagination. She moaned as she felt her knees weaken and her grip on his shoulders tightened.

He felt her unspoken surrender, and it blasted into his senses simply because it was so unexpected. He felt confused—because this was

*Natasha* he was kissing. Natasha whose sleek curves he could feel beneath his seeking fingers. Natasha who was inciting him to the kind of kiss which only led to one place, and that place was bed. And Raffaele knew that if he didn't stop doing what he was doing then she was going to get a whole lot more than she had bargained for.

He tore his mouth away from hers, the thunder of his heart seeming to drown the sound of traffic which hummed in the nearby street. Her lips were still parted, wet from where he had licked them, and the pale blue of her eyes was almost completely obscured by the blackness of desire. He felt some strange feeling overpower him—more anger than frustration— as if he had been just playing with her and she had damned well played him back at his own game. So, was she sexually more experienced than she let on? Her quiet evenings nothing more than a bluff for when he happened to be in residence?

Natasha stared up at him, her kiss-crushed mouth trembling, trying and failing to read that dangerously wild, dark glint in his eyes. 'Why did…why did you do that?' she whispered.

Why, indeed? To punish her for the crime of

making him want her when she was out of bounds? Or for having worked too effective a transformation from housekeeper to wife-in-waiting? Or maybe because he couldn't ever remember wanting to kiss a woman that badly in a long time?

But all this was a pretence, he told himself furiously, and maybe they both needed to be reminded of that fact.

His autocratic mouth curved into a close approximation of a smile, but it stayed light-years away from his eyes. 'Didn't you know that there's a journalist hiding nearby, sniffing around for a story? And I think we may have provided him with one,' he whispered, steeling his heart to the dawning hurt in her eyes. 'What a pity there wasn't a camera to hand!'

For a moment, she thought he was joking, but one look at his mocking face made her realise he was deadly serious and she began to try to wriggle out of his arms. But Raffaele's grip was too firm for her to be able to move away effectively. In fact, all it was doing was… Her eyes widened.

'*Si*,' he said grimly. 'You feel it? You feel me? What you do to me? How much you make me want you?'

'Let…me…*go!*' she breathed.

'But you should not kiss a man like that if you are not prepared to take the consequences!'

'You…you *bastard!*'

But now the spark of fire in her eyes was doing the impossible, turning him on even more, and he wondered why the hell that should be—until he realised that her usual role in his life was docility. Suddenly, she had stepped out from behind that role and he found himself wondering what else he might find beneath.

'Shh, *cara,*' he said softly. 'We don't want that nice journalist to think we are rowing, do we? Not when we are about to tell the world we're engaged.'

'Will you let me go?'

'In a minute.' But still he held her, unable to relinquish the softness of her body as he willed the exquisite pain of desire to subside. He felt her relax against him, heard her soft sigh of submission and saw her eyes briefly close in surrender. '*Si,*' he whispered. 'This is the way of it. You see how helpless we all can be, Natasha—held in thrall to our most primitive longings? You and I, we choose to play a game—to concoct an elaborate masquerade— but underneath it all we are just a man and a woman, programmed by nature to join together in the most fundamental way possible.'

But, oh, how that hurt. That almost *anatomical* dissection of their kiss, which was poles apart from her crazy longings. If anything could have painted a picture of just how heartless Raffaele de Feretti really was, then his words had done it with perfect clarity.

'Will you let me go?' she whispered.

'I will.' He snaked his tongue out over his dry lips and his eyes sparked with provocation, but the ache in his body was real enough—as was his fleeting sense of regret that this *was* a game. That he couldn't just haul her upstairs and let this mad desire burn itself out in a few hours of delicious sex. 'Unless you want one last kiss before I do?' he murmured.

The awful thing was that she *did*—even though he had done it just to give the reporter an eyeful! But it was—as he had gone to great pains to remind her—nothing but a physical hunger. It wasn't something rooted in the emotions—well, certainly not in his—and she mustn't forget that. *I don't want to end up being badly hurt,* she thought fiercely, and this time she *did* pull away.

'No, thank you,' she said. 'I'd like to see

Sam—and then to hang all these beautiful clothes up before they get too creased.'

Anger carried her along to flounce past him, enjoying his faintly bemused expression as she left him to carry in all her bags. Let him wait on *her* for a change, she thought!

But inside, her negative feelings dissolved into love as she found Sam fast asleep in the garden room, as Raffaele had said. In front of him ran a film showing *The World's Greatest Ever Goals*— her little boy was football-mad, and didn't Raffaele occasionally take him to see a match on one of those rare Saturdays when he was free?

She stood and watched his snuggled little form, feeling a huge lump constricting her throat, knowing that one day soon she was going to have to take her child away from a man he had grown to love—almost like a father. But Raffaele *wasn't* his father, and what choice did she have but to leave? To grow old before her time in this house, not living at all except in his formidable shadow—what example would *that* be to set for her young son?

She touched her fingers to his soft cheek. 'Wake up,' she said softly. Wake up, darling.'

Sleepily, Sam blinked up to her. 'You look different, Mama.'

'Mama's had her hair cut, that's why.' And Mama's wearing fine clothes and underwear. All paid for with Raffaele's money. She felt the stain of guilt flare into her cheeks. 'Are you hungry?'

'No,' he said absently, and then murmured something in Italian, as he often did if he'd spent a protracted period of time with Raffaele. Usually, she delighted in how he could practise his language skills, but today all it served to do was to emphasise the advantages that this life gave him—advantages which would swiftly disappear, like a bubble popping, once she left the Italian's employment.

Raffaele walked in the room and saw her lean over to tenderly brush a lock of hair away from the boy's head—but it was as if he was looking at someone he'd never met before. Yes, she was an exemplary mother and a reliable worker— yet, today, it was as if someone had waved a magic wand and made her into someone else. Where was the Natasha he knew?

He had brusquely told her that his taste in women was exacting—but he had not in his wildest dreams believed that she could have so magnificently become the very embodiment of his ideal woman. Was this going to complicate matters? Mercilessly, he quelled the raw rush of desire, knowing that he couldn't afford to let it.

But then his phone rang, and Raffaele went out of the room to answer it. It was Troy, and he sounded both bemused and pleased.

'I've just had the *Daily View* on the line, saying that you've been spotted kissing a glamorous blonde outside the house and they want a comment,' he said. 'What's going on, Raffaele? This is pretty confusing. I thought that it was Natasha who was going to be the decoy— though you know I always had my reservations about her ability to carry it off. So who is it? Who's the mystery woman?

'There is no mystery,' said Raffaele, with a beat of satisfaction whose source he did not recognise. 'The woman was Natasha.'

There was a stunned silence. *'Natasha?'*

'Yes, Natasha,' Raffaele answered coolly. 'As for a comment—there is none. But you might like to mention that I shall be taking the glamorous blonde in question to a charity dinner on Monday night.' His voice dipped. 'And she will be wearing my engagement ring.'

# CHAPTER SIX

'NATASHA!'

She could hear the note of impatience in his voice.

'Natasha!' he called again.

'I'll be two seconds, Raffaele!' she called down, and turned back to her son.

Sam was sitting before an open drawing book at the little desk in his room, silvering the stars which were sprinkled through a unicorn's mane. 'Good night, darling,' she said—feeling as if she were proposing to leave him for a month, instead of just one evening.

''Night, Mama,' he murmured, and smiled. 'You look nice.'

She didn't feel *nice*. She felt like a fraud— or whatever the feminine equivalent of a wolf all done up in sheep's clothing was. Natasha shivered. And she was *cold*—unused to having such large areas of flesh on show, even though she knew that other women would wear dresses such as these to the charity ball she and Raffaele were due to attend that night.

'You're sure you don't mind being left with the babysitter?' she asked anxiously, as she had asked him several times since supper. It occurred to Natasha that if Sam had been a more manipulative child then he might have said that, yes, he did mind, that he wasn't used to his mother leaving him with other people—and demand that she stay behind. And wasn't there a part of her that would have been hugely relieved to have done just that? Surely, just *being* Raffaele's fiancée would be enough to fool people—without them having to turn up and appear at parties like a pair of performing seals?

Sam shook his head. 'No, I like Anna. She's fun. She sings songs into a hairbrush!'

Natasha forced a smile. 'Does she?' The drama student daughter of some people down the road was certainly lively—and she adored Sam—but it was the first time Natasha had ever used her. Would she be able to detect a fire if one started in the basement? Or would she use this opportunity to import a load of unsuitable friends, leaving Sam forgotten while she partied?

Telling herself that her own nervousness was

being transmitted into worrying about her son, Natasha set off downstairs, where Anna was waiting in the hall, talking to Raffaele. They both looked up as Natasha carefully began to descend the wide and sweeping staircase—still finding the scarlet patent shoes a little high and her dress a little long—the red silk gown making soft whispering sounds as it slithered down to the ground around her.

It seemed to take for ever to get to the bottom, especially with Raffaele's eyes fixed on her like that—an ebony spotlight which spilled over her with dark light. 'Here I am,' she said brightly.

There was a heartbeat of a pause. 'So I see.' Raffaele's gaze was steady as he watched her unaccustomed movements. He was used to seeing Natasha in jeans and trainers, striding around the place at a fast pace, but this Natasha moved differently—probably because of those killer heels she was wearing. If he stopped to listen carefully enough, would he hear the silken sound of her thighs brushing together? And was she wearing stockings underneath that bright waterfall of a dress? He felt a pulse spring to life deep in his groin.

'Wow—you look *amazing,* Natasha!' said Anna. 'I can't believe it's you!'

'I know the feeling,' said Natasha wryly, relieved to have reached the bottom of the stairs without tumbling over.

'Come here, over to the light, and let me look at you properly,' murmured Raffaele.

He stepped back to survey her, one hand cupping his elbow, a forefinger pressed to his lips—in exactly the way people did when they were studying a painting in an art gallery. *As if I'm on show,* thought Natasha indignantly, *as if I'm a possession*—until she reminded herself that there was no point in being indignant. She had known exactly what she was getting into. This was exactly what it was supposed to be. A game.

So play it. She tipped her head slightly, feeling the heavy mass of her hair, which was piled high in an elaborate confection courtesy of a hairdresser who had arrived earlier this evening for just that purpose. The circle of platinum around her finger felt heavy, too—as if her slender hands were too fragile to cope with the weight of such a colossal gem, and the imbalance was threatening to make her topple and fall.

Deciding that to go and shop for a ring like normal mortals would be too crass in light of the exceptional circumstances, Raffaele had sent out for the jewels in the way that other people might send out for a takeaway! A tray of engagement rings had been brought to the house in a window-darkened car which had housed two hefty bodyguards as well as the jeweller and gem expert. Before he had ordered a selection Raffaele had demanded to know which stones she would like to look at.

'I don't really know,' she'd blustered.

Raffaele had frowned. 'You must have *some* idea?'

'Why should I? It's not something I've ever given a lot of thought to.'

'No?' His voice had been frankly disbelieving. 'I thought that all women dreamed of engagement rings?'

For once, Natasha's gaze was genuinely cold. Of all the arrogant assertions he could have made—that was possibly the most offensive! 'Maybe in your circles they do!' she retorted.

'Oh, they do.' He gave a cynical laugh. 'Most certainly they do.'

Oddly enough, that made Natasha think. Of course he was eligible—she didn't have to see the articles in all the glossies to know *that*—but she had always thought that he would be liked…loved…for sheer charisma alone. But Raffaele had power and prestige, as well as a

hard body and the face of a fallen angel—
wouldn't that make *any* woman want him?
Enough to plot to get him? she wondered. She
felt her heart softening, wanting to defend him
against such scheming women—until she reminded herself that Raffaele was well able to
look after himself.

'No, you choose,' she said evasively, because
there was part of her that wanted nothing to do
with the ring. It was a prop, she reminded
herself—nothing more. If she started telling
him that she liked one gem more than another,
if she started investing it with her likes and
dislikes, then it would assume an importance
which would be unnecessary. More as a de-
fence mechanism than anything—Natasha
didn't want to become in any way attached to
a meaningless bauble—she bit back the infor-
mation that she had always rather liked aqua-
marines and insisted that he decide.

Yet wasn't it a very feminine reaction to be
disappointed when he opted for a diamond? For
its cold, precious fire seemed so totally lacking
in feeling. It was a huge, pear-shaped stone of
a seriously significant carat-size—according to
the jeweller.

'It's a good investment, *Signor* de Feretti.'

Raffaele had turned to her. 'Do you like it, *cara?*'

Did he see her wince at the jeweller's crass observation? And was she supposed to go through the pantomime of dazed fiancée as he slipped it on to her finger? Apparently, she was.

'It's magnificent,' she said truthfully.

And now, tonight's charity ball was the ring's first outing—and *their* first outing as a couple.

Raffaele slipped the velvet evening wrap around her shivering shoulders, his fingertips brushing against her pale smooth flesh, and he noticed how dark his skin looked against hers. Unbidden and unwanted, came another image—the one which couldn't seem to stop burning itself with searing clarity into the fevered recesses of his mind. Of his hard dark body pinning down her submissive milky whiteness. Of running his hands and his tongue over every curve she possessed.

Beneath the exquisitely cut evening trousers Raffaele felt the ache of sexual hunger—surprising in its intensity. Was that because he knew he couldn't have her? Because she was not his equal and to take her to his bed would be to take advantage of her—was that her sudden inexplicable lure for him? Surely, to a man who had every-thing, the forbidden would have a powerful lure all of its own.

'The car is here,' he said huskily.

Outside the night was clear, the indigo sky star-sprinkled, and Raffaele could see the faint cloud of his warm breath against the cold air as he watched her get into the back of the limousine.

'So, do you like going to these kind of dos?' asked Natasha, as he slid onto the backseat beside her.

'They serve a purpose.'

'You mean, they raise money for charity?'

In the darkness he gave a brief half-smile. How genuinely innocent she was in the ways of the world he inhabited. 'Something like that.'

'What else?' she persisted—because they had to talk about *something* if they were going to get through this evening.

He turned to her. The shadows and the flick-ered illumination from the passing streetlamps were playing interesting combinations of light and shade on her face. Her lips glistened with unaccustomed lipstick and her eyes looked huge, almost startled. This new Natasha was taking some getting used to.

'You don't want to know,' he murmured.

'Keep your sweet, idealistic view, Natasha—believe me, it's a rare quality.'

Idealism was all very well—but not if it meant you were always on the outside, looking in. 'I want to learn,' she said stubbornly. 'I might as well get something out of the experience.'

Surprisingly, her comment wounded him—though whether it was just his pride which was hurt, he wasn't quite sure. Raffaele gave a short laugh. Maybe it served him right. What did he expect? Fluttering gratitude at all times of the day? 'Okay, then, I'll teach you all about the big, bad world. Yes, of course these events raise money for worthy causes—but, for a lot of people, it's important to be *seen* to be giving.'

'But not to you?'

His eyes narrowed. 'Was that a question or a statement? Should I be flattered or offended?'

Natasha might have been worried about the evening ahead and feeling out of her depth, but she always tried to be scrupulously fair and she shook her head. 'I don't think you need your ego bolstered by other people's opinions of you.'

'Why, thank you, Natasha,' he murmured.

The look which washed over her filled her with ridiculous pleasure and, quickly, she turned to look out of the window, afraid that he might see. It was important that he didn't. He must not see how vulnerable she was to his praise. She had already let herself down by responding to his kiss like that—much more and he might begin to guess at her feelings for him. And then what?

Wouldn't he be appalled? Embarrassed? Even outraged that she had dared to presume to nurture longings for a man like him?

'Here we are,' he murmured, his voice butting into her thoughts. 'Now, take a deep breath before you prepare to enter into the fray, *cara*.'

Natasha peered out of the window at the dazzling sight which awaited them. The venue was one of London's most glitzy hotels, its exterior bright with lights so that it looked as if there was a whole galaxy of stars burning at the front of its upmarket site opposite Hyde Park.

A roped-off red carpet made a startling red river and, on either side, were banks of photographers with huge and rather intimidating lenses which looked like alien eyes. Natasha sucked in a breath. Could she really go through with this?

Raffaele saw the way she had stiffened, and he tilted his dark head. 'Are you sure you're ready for this, Natasha?'

She was tempted to say that she wasn't. That

she was hopelessly miscast for this role and no one would ever believe that a man like Raffaele de Feretti would have proposed marriage to someone like her.

But if she backed out now, then wouldn't she always be left feeling some kind of wimpish failure, as well as letting Raffaele down horribly at the very last moment? Shouldn't she just seize on this as a glamorous adventure—a taste of real luxury which she could store in her memory bank?

Turning a little, she shook her head and smiled. 'I'm as ready as a woman could possibly be!' she said.

He thought that if it had been any other woman looking like that in the backseat of the car then by now he would have kissed her and touched her—why, they might even have…

'Raffaele!'

'Mmm?' His erotic daydream shattered.

'The chauffeur is holding the door open,' she scolded.

Adjusting his jacket and trying to quell the dull ache of frustration, Raffaele got out of the car first and then held his hand out for hers. Her left hand. The one with the ring on it.

Natasha trembled as the massive diamond

caught the light, It seemed to flash and sparkle with the significance of a beacon shining on top of an isolated lighthouse. But the wearing of this ring was simply to send out a message—it was not a symbol of how two people felt about each other.

The press went wild.

'Natasha! Hey, Natasha! Look this way!'

'Over here, Natasha!'

Countless flashbulbs exploded—bleaching the night with blinding white light so that Natasha blinked and swayed a little. Raffaele's hand tightened on her elbow.

'You okay?' he murmured, his head distractingly close to hers.

More flashbulbs exploded.

'I'm…fine. Just a little dazzled.' She wobbled back a smile. 'Literally!'

It occurred to him that Natasha could be witty and clever even during a stressful occasion like this—or was that the most insufferably patronising thing to think? Had he forgotten that she'd been midway through a degree when she'd become pregnant with Sam? He frowned. And that women's lives were changed by having babies in a way that men's never were.

'Come on,' he said, his voice suddenly raw

and he wondered why the hell he was concentrating on inconsequential things like *that* when he had a whole evening of subterfuge to get through. He slipped his hand around the silken span of her waist in an unashamedly proprietorial gesture, spanning his fingers out to increase the area of her body he was touching, and realised that he was enjoying it. He was enjoying it very much.

'Raffaele!' someone shrieked. 'What made you want to marry your housekeeper?'

'Natasha!' shrieked another, as if they had known her all their lives. 'What's it like being engaged to a billionaire?'

'Just keep smiling,' he murmured. 'Don't say a thing.'

'I wasn't intending to.'

Once inside the foyer, which was filled with blooms so scented that momentarily Natasha felt quite faint, different members of staff converged on them like well-oiled parts of a huge machine.

'Can I take your wrap, madam?'

She slipped it from her shoulders and handed it over to the female member of staff, unused to the deference she was being shown. And, suddenly, she identified far more with the girl in uniform than with the glamorous creatures who were milling around, laughing as if they had all been let in on some secret and fabulously funny joke. *I'm just like you!* she found herself wanting to say to the smiling girl.

Without the silk-velvet cloak Natasha felt bare and exposed—and as Raffaele led her into the chandelier-bright ballroom she realised that she was. Exposed to the lenses of the cameras outside, and now exposed to the penetrating gazes of the women within the spectacular interior of the room.

Were her nerves so on edge that she imagined the faint murmur of comment? No. And neither was there anything the matter with her vision. She saw the heads turn and gazes look her over—from head to toe.

'Okay?' questioned Raffaele, for he'd felt her tense beneath his hand.

She wasn't—not really. But neither was she going to give up at the first hurdle. 'Suddenly, I can identify with exhibits at the zoo!'

'It's that bad?' There was a sudden gleam of understanding in the jet-dark eyes. 'You need a drink.'

Did she? Maybe she did. 'Thanks.'

Taking two flutes of champagne from a passing waitress, he handed her one, and, as

Natasha raised it to her lips, the bubbles fizzed up her nose. She wrinkled it.

'You are not used to champagne,' he commented.

'Don't patronise me, Raffaele,' she remonstrated softly as she drank some and thought how dry it tasted.

'I'm not. It was an observation, not a criticism.'

'Of course I'm not used to it. I don't come from a champagne-drinking background—more the glass-of-wine-at-Christmas type. I drank some for the first time at university—but it certainly wasn't anything like this stuff.' She shrugged, wondering why the hell she had taken the conversation down to this particular dead-end. 'The bubbly I drank wasn't real champagne.'

'Was that with Sam's father?' he demanded, seeing the way her features had become shuttered and finding himself suddenly—inexplicably—wanting to know.

He had never asked her anything like that before, and it occurred to her that now was not the right time.

'Yes, it was,' she said, her cheeks flaring with the memory. But she was saved from saying any more by a couple bearing down on them. Nervously, she drank a little more champagne, fleetingly thinking that maybe she *could* see what the fuss was all about. It really was *very* moreish!

'Raffaele! So this is why you have such a fearsome reputation as a poker player! You have a beautiful woman like this tucked away at home—and nobody's ever seen her!'

The immaculately groomed man who spoke looked as if he was in his fifties, but the woman with him was about half that age—more like Natasha's. She, too, had an expensive-looking head of blonde hair and a silken dress which clung to her firm, lush young body. Had she always looked like that? Natasha wondered. Or had she, too, been subjected to the perfect makeover courtesy of someone else's money?

Natasha suddenly had a horrible feeling of predictability—as if she had just been plucked off a production line of eager wannabes. Was that what other people thought of *her*—that she had bargained away her youth and her rather lowly position to be at the beck and call of a wealthy man?

Except that Raffaele is only in his thirties, she reminded herself. And it wasn't his *money* she was interested in. Biting her lip, she swallowed some more champagne. It wasn't her place to be interested in him at all!

'Yes, this is Natasha,' Raffaele was saying. 'Natasha, meet John Huntingdon—he and I have done a little business together.'

'A little business?' laughed John, as he shook her hand. 'He bought my office block in Canary Wharf!'

Raffaele was now narrowing his eyes at the blonde. 'I'm sorry—I don't think we've met?'

The blonde gave Raffaele a fluttery smile which matched her fluttery voice. 'No, we haven't—I'd certainly have remembered *you!* Hi, I'm Susi.'

'Hello, Susi,' said Raffaele gravely.

'Congratulations!' Susi had now turned her attention to Natasha, picking up her hand and looking at the ring with barely disguised greed. 'You must tell me how you did it—I've been trying to get John to buy me a sparkler for—'

'Oh, all of three months,' put in John smoothly. 'In fact, almost from the moment we met! Anyway, we're all on the same table—so we'll see you in a little while.' He placed his hand in the small of Susi's back and propelled her forward, like a horse who was refusing to jump. 'Come along, darling—there's a good girl.'

Natasha felt slightly humiliated on the other woman's behalf—but hadn't she rather set it up for herself, by playing the part of gold-digger whilst flirting with Raffaele? And now more people were coming over, flocking round them like ants to a dollop of spilled jam, and she suddenly experienced a frightening feeling of vulnerability as they were surrounded by curious eyes.

Natasha was glad to sit down for dinner—though she had little appetite for the seemingly endless array of tiny but luxurious dishes which kept appearing in front of her. Quite honestly, the dress was cut so close to her figure that anything more than a morsel would have made it uncomfortable to sit in. No wonder these women managed to stay so thin!

Candles flickered and perfect white flowers cast their heady scent over the select gathering. John Huntingdon sat on one side of her and a corporate lawyer named Charles on the other. All the men at the table seemed to be headhunters, or something to do with finance—not really Natasha's area of expertise at all.

Everyone seemed to belong—as if they were all members of the same exclusive club who all went to the same events on the city's star-studded social calendar.

'How come I haven't seen you before? You weren't at Wimbledon?' one of the women asked Natasha.

She admitted she hadn't been.

'Oh! What about Cheltenham?'

'That's a horse race, *cara mia,*' Raffaele enlightened her in a wry voice as he saw her frown.

Fleetingly, she thought how ironic it was that this Italian should know more about England than she did. Because it's not your world, she reminded herself. It never has been, and that simple fact is not about to change.

As Raffaele watched her he thought how *sweet* she looked. And how simple—for all her expensive clothes and the ludicrously large ring which completely dwarfed her slender hand. Whereas the other women had the definition of gym-worked muscle, which rippled rather unattractively against the silks and chiffons, Natasha's physique came from running round after Sam, or going from the top to the bottom of the house with a vacuum cleaner in hand.

Even after her glossy transformation she still had some quality about her which marked her out. Some stillness—almost a purity. She looked, he thought, like a flower which had been picked from somebody's garden—all soft and natural and a complete contrast to the scentless perfection of the hothouse blooms which surrounded them.

His mouth hardened. What was this cynic thinking? Was he projecting some kind of wishful fairytale onto this particular woman because they inhabited different worlds? It was easy to fantasise about someone when you knew that reality would never be allowed to intrude to shatter it.

Yet you wanted her when you kissed her, didn't you? *And—more than that——you wanted to pin her down somewhere and to thrust into her until you had lost yourself.*

He barely tasted the fine wines and the food was unremarkable—despite the cost and the lavish attention paid to its preparation. But Raffaele wasn't hungry.

He glanced across the table at Natasha again—it seemed that she had overcome her initial shyness and was now nodding intently at something the man opposite her was saying. She said something to John Huntingdon, who was sitting beside her, and Raffaele was surprised and not pleased to see both men laughing.

He felt the unfamiliar thump of jealousy—bizarre and inexplicable—and instead of inwardly groaning at the sound of the orchestra, which was just starting up, he found himself rising to his feet to walk round table and hold out his hand proprietorially.

'Dance with me.'

As so often with Raffaele, it was an order and not a request, but that didn't stop Natasha excusing herself to the people she'd been talking to. Because, even if Raffaele hadn't been her boss and even if they hadn't been masquerading to the world as a newly engaged couple, she just wanted to dance with him.

She had been trying her best not to feast her eyes on him during the meal, but she hadn't made very much headway, blown away by the knee-weakening vision he made in formal evening wear. Black suited him. Well, everything seemed to suit him—but black especially so. It accentuated the charcoal depths of his hair and his eyes and contrasted with the golden-olive glow of his skin. There were many men there tonight—all of them rich and well-connected—but there was not another in the entire ballroom who could have held a candle to her Raffaele.

'I'd love to,' she responded softly, 'seeing as you asked so nicely!'

Raffaele's eyes narrowed as he led her onto the floor—the only time he could remember ever being first up to dance. Was she…*teasing* him? Was she perhaps taking this whole subterfuge a little far—responding to him as his *equal?*

But all thoughts evaporated into insignificance when he pulled her against him. She felt…well, *sconosciuta*…strange—and not just because it was a brand-new woman in his arms. They began to move in time with the music.

With Natasha he felt acutely aware of her body. Of the undulation of her waist as he wound his fingers around it, sinuously as a snake. Of the light brush of her breasts against his chest, the knowledge that her amazing bottom was so tantalisingly close. That he could reach out his hands and cup it with possessive anticipation, then grind her hips towards his, so that she could feel for herself the hard ache of desire which was threatening to—

He groaned, experiencing a confusing mixture of wanting the forbidden and yet being confronted with the sweetly familiar. Had he thought this was going to be easy? Of course he had.

'It's…it's a fantastic band,' said Natasha,

sensing his tension and feeling more than a little tense herself. He felt so good. He smelt so good. She found that she wanted to reach up on tiptoe and whisper her lips over the dark curve of his jaw. Beneath the thin silk of her evening gown she could feel the wild, uncontrollable flutter of her heart. Unseen, with her cheek close to the dark shoulder of his dinner jacket, she whispered. 'Isn't it?'

What the hell was she talking about? Ah, yes—the music. He wished it wasn't there—for he would have preferred to have listened to the soft sigh of her breath and the heavy beat of her heart. The music of her body as it began to play out the familiar melody of desire.

He found that he wanted to press his body against hers, to slide his hard thigh between the giving softness of hers. And, yet, while such a display of intimacy might almost be expected of a couple who had just announced their betrothal, he knew that he could not do it. If it was anyone other than Natasha then, yes—he could pretend. But the game might get out of hand and, if it did, then wouldn't he be tempted to do it properly, to make love to her? And that really *would* be taking advantage of her subservient position in the most despicable way possible.

'I'm bored with dancing,' he said curtly. 'Let's break, shall we? Do you mind?

Natasha shook her head as he led her off the dance-floor. *Or does he really mean that he's bored with me?* she wondered, somehow managing to stop her smile from slipping. But this isn't about *you,* she reminded herself. Ultimately, it's about Elisabetta.

He caught her by the arm, his fingers gripping into her soft flesh. He saw the way her eyes widened as they searched his face anxiously——and something about her concern put him on the defensive. Why the hell were they still here? Hadn't they done enough for their diversionary plan to succeed? 'I can't face any more sitting around that table and making small talk.'

'I thought you were discussing deals—*I* was the one making small talk!'

'So I saw. You seemed to have all the men round the table eating out of your hand.' His mouth hardened into a determined line. 'So why don't we just leave quietly, before anyone actually notices we're gone?'

As if no one would notice that Raffaele de Feretti was no longer in their presence! 'Won't they think it rude?' Natasha asked, turning her face up to his.

'They'll think it perfectly understandable for us to want a little time on our own,' he clipped out, because when her lips parted with innocent question he wanted to crush them beneath his.

'Okay, then—but I really think we ought to say goodbye first,' said Natasha stubbornly.

He opened his mouth to tell her that what *she* wanted was irrelevant, but to his astonishment she was already walking away from him, the taut curves of her bottom drawing his eye irresistibly as she made her way back to the table.

# CHAPTER SEVEN

OUTSIDE, the press had multiplied like bacteria, and two heavy-looking security men had to clear them a path to the waiting car.

'Blame yourself!' Raffaele snapped, as he pushed Natasha into the back of the limousine and then jumped in behind her, slamming the door on the jostling pack as it moved away.

'Wh-why?' Natasha didn't like to ask him to move his thigh from where it was pressing against hers—not when his eyes were spitting irritated black fire at her.

'You went around saying goodbye to everyone like they were long-lost friends, meaning that someone got word out to the press that we were leaving!'

'It was just good manners,' said Natasha, her determination to remain cheerful at all costs evaporating under the onslaught of his quite unreasonable display of temper. And there was still that leg, of course.

He could hardly believe what she had said. 'You think that I...*I* need a lesson in manners?'

She stared right back. He thought he was immune to criticism, did he? 'Right now, yes. Yes, I do!'

'From you?'

'Why not from me?' she retorted furiously. 'If I'm good enough to be engaged to you and brought here on your arm, then I'm reckon I'm good enough for just about anything else!'

'Oh, you do?'

'Yes, I do!'

There was a heartbeat of a pause.

'Good enough to kiss, perhaps?' he questioned deliberately.

The confined atmosphere of the car closed in on them. The hungry flash of warning in his eyes. The gleam of his lips. And still the warm, hard pressure of his thigh. She should have seen it coming. She wanted to say *Raffaele, please don't do this!*

And she wanted to beg him to just do it— *and do it now.*

'Raffaele,' she breathed, her voice low and husky and complicit.

' *"Raffaele!"* ' he mimicked, almost harshly—for she had him in her power, something he had not anticipated nor prepared for, and she would now taste the consequence of that for herself. He was going to kiss her, and it was wrong, more than wrong—she knew that and he knew that. But—*Madonna mia*—he was going to do it all the same!

With a throaty sound halfway between a groan and a tiny roar, he pulled her unprotesting body into his arms, his hands digging into her sweet, yielding flesh and drove his mouth down on hers in a kiss that was filled with anger as much as lust.

With an answering cry of need Natasha fell back against the skin-soft leather seat of the car. His hands were on the bare flesh of her back, his lips coaxing hers open—while that rogue thigh was pushing its way insistently between hers. She shivered with violent need. She knew she should stop him and, yet, nothing could have made her call a halt to the debilitating sweetness of that kiss.

Trying to ignore the doubts which were flaring in her mind, Natasha took his hard and proud face in her hands, cupping its sculpted shield shape as if to reassure herself it was real. That he was real. That this was really happening.

Oh, but it was.

With a gasp, her hands fell away at the precise moment that his fingers grazed over her nipple—so hard it was almost painful, pushing against the silk-satin of her evening dress as if it wanted to be free of the constricting gown. And as if he had read her thoughts, he slipped the delicate strap of her gown down over her shoulder, so that her breast was bare. She felt first warm air against the naked skin, and then—shockingly—the flick of his mouth on it.

Shuddering, she looked down—and there was Raffaele's dark head, suckling her. And that shockingly intimate touch jarred the growing voice of her conscience even as her body silently screamed out its answering desire. *This isn't right,* she told herself frantically. *You know it isn't. Especially in the back of a car!*

She tasted sweet. She tasted salty. She tasted of woman and of need. Raffaele was nearly exploding as his tongue played with the puckering bud, and he felt her squirm beneath his hands, heard her tiny gasps of pleasure. It was so unexpected. So *bizarre.* In a few short days the woman who brought him tea in the afternoons had been transformed into this passionate creature who was writhing around in his arms!

He felt the hard need of his desire pressing against him. If it had been anyone else but Natasha he would have guided her hand there. She would have unzipped him. Taken him into her mouth…

*What the hell was he thinking of?*

He didn't care. It didn't matter. Nothing mattered except—

'Raffaele!' Sanity prevailed for the single instant it took Natasha to push at his chest, the word indistinct because it took every bit of determination for her to say it.

But the muffled protest was like being showered with icy water. With a groan, Raffaele tore his mouth away from her, letting go of her as if she had suddenly become contaminated. He slid over to the opposite side of the seat, steadying his ragged breathing, his pounding heart.

She waited until she had pulled her dress back up before she risked a glance at him, and she bit her lip, sensing his anger. Yet she'd *had* to stop what was happening. Surely, he realised that. 'Raffaele?'

He turned his head then, and Natasha almost recoiled at the icy look of detachment in his eyes. 'What?'

What had Kirsty told her to acquire along with her brand-new wardrobe? Attitude—that was it.

'That…well, that shouldn't have happened,' she said coolly.

He looked at her almost with admiration. How effortlessly she had slipped into the role of fiancée! 'You think I don't know that?' he growled softly, and yet he was aware that something remarkable had happened. A woman had stopped Raffaele de Feretti from making love to her. When had *that* ever happened before? His mouth became a grim line of realisation. *In nessun momento*—never!

And while his pride and his ego made him want to capture her in his arms and kiss her again, in a way that would leave her gasping and reeling and *begging* him to do it to her, infuriatingly, he could see that she had made the right decision. 'You think I want to complicate further this damned ridiculous situation?' he snapped. 'By adolescent fumbling in the back of a car? That certainly wasn't included in the deal!'

She was about to say that she didn't think any particular *deal* had been hammered out—but perhaps he was referring to his offer that she could keep the costly ring? More hurtful was to hear that mind-blowing kiss dismissed in such a careless way.

'Do you always kiss women like that?' she demanded.

He gave an arrogant smile. 'What do you think?' he challenged softly. Was her *ego* growing at the same pace as her ease with her new role? 'Do you think I turn on simply for *you?*'

His mocking tone tore into her. But she was damned if she was going to show him that he'd hurt her—because he might just start to question why.

'Obviously not,' she said smoothly. 'You don't get a reputation as a superstud unless it's well founded.'

He stared at her, outraged, scarcely able to believe what he'd heard. *'Superstud?'* he repeated dangerously.

How formidable the feeling of getting your own back could be—and what a marvellous way of distracting her aching body from the sweet pleasures she had denied it. He had wounded her and now he was having a taste of his own medicine.

'Oh, come on, Raffaele,' she protested. 'You are listed and photographed in the international gossip columns with a series of glamorous women on your arm—some of whom have actually gone on record to boast about your sexual prowess. If that isn't being a superstud, then I don't know what is!'

There was complete silence apart from the quiet thrum of the car's powerful engine, and Raffaele was so livid at her assessment that, for once in his life, he couldn't think of a thing to say. But that didn't last long, and he turned to her, his eyes spitting dark fire.

'You think that I am defined by my ability to pleasure women—like some kind of *gigolo?*'

She had never seen him look quite so indignant and, in spite of everything, Natasha burst out laughing.

'What's so funny?' he demanded furiously.

'You are! Of course I'm not calling you a gigolo—I don't expect you've ever had to pay for sex in your life—'

'Natasha!' he put in warningly.

But she blazed on. 'People say things when they're…' *When they're* what, *Natasha?* When they're head-over-heels in love with a man who sees them just as an object in their lives? So quit while you're ahead. Show him that it's no big deal. But was she really that good an actress?

'There's no need to overreact, Raffaele,' she finished softly.

Oh, wasn't there? Did she have any idea of how much he was aching for her right now? How if he wasn't such a gentleman he would be sliding that dress up her thighs right now and letting his fingers entice her. He swallowed, made a barely perceptible curse. The irony did not escape him—even at such a moment of high desire—that no one had ever accused Raffaele de Feretti of being a gentleman before, least of all himself!

Yet, infuriatingly, she was right. There were two ways this could go—and the most obvious one would certainly be the easiest and most pleasurable to carry through. He could carry on kissing her, and she could carry on responding, and things would inevitably progress to the next stage of having sex with her. Maybe not in the back of the car—but certainly when they got back to the house.

But think of all the complications that would throw up along the way. How would they both feel about it in the morning, when the heat of passion had been vanquished and sated? When she had to go and get Sam his cereal and take him to school as if nothing had happened? Then what? He wanted them to play-act at being engaged—but that would be taking method-acting one stage too far!

No, the most rational thing to do, under these circumstances, was to put it down to a cocktail of proximity and the raging hormones of two people in their sexual prime.

Raffaele scowled. When was he going to stop thinking in this crazy way? This was *Natasha,* and he needed to remember that. Maybe he should tell her to get changed into her ordinary clothes as soon as they were home—to make him a pot of decaffeinated coffee, the way she always did when he arrived home late.

It had been she who had insisted on the decaf, he remembered rather inconsequentially—after she'd once commented that he'd looked tired and he had confessed to lack of sleep. It had been during the Palladio takeover, he remembered, and frowned.

Crossing one long leg over the other, relieved to see the end of his street, he decided that maybe such a request wouldn't be the wisest course of action. There was no way of second-guessing how she might react. The old Natasha seemed to have disappeared—lost in her brand-new hairstyle and her brand-new and overly provocative wardrobe. Would he ever get her back? he wondered.

Once again, he scowled. 'We're here,' he said flatly, as the car drew to a halt.

She got out of the car before the driver had time to open the door for her. *I'm off-duty now,* she thought defiantly as she walked up to the front door and let herself in.

Anna was curled up in the television room, reading a weighty looking book on mime and dance, and she looked up when Natasha walked in, and smiled.

'Oh, you're back earlier than I thought. Did you have a good evening?'

'It was fantastic,' said Natasha, with the kind of enthusiasm she thought would be expected of her.

Anna frowned. 'You look a bit pale,' she commented.

'I'm just tired,' said Natasha lamely.

'Mmm. Me, too,' came a voice as smooth as honeyed cream, and Raffaele walked straight over to her and slid his hand possessively around her.

Half in alarm, Natasha looked up to see a sensual glint in the ebony eyes, and her heart began to pound in spite of everything.

'I guess it's an early night for us, *mia bella,*'

he murmured, and began to teasingly caress the indentation at her waist.

'Oh, I *quite* understand!' said Anna, jumping to her feet and grinning.

With a tight smile, Natasha shook herself free of his embrace and walked over to Anna. 'Sam's okay?' she questioned.

'Sam's fine. I read him two stories and then he fell asleep. I haven't heard a peep out of him once!'

'I'll walk you home,' said Raffaele.

'No, please. It's just down the road!' protested Anna. 'Honestly, I'm a big girl now—you should see where I live during term-time.'

'I'll walk you,' he repeated obdurately.

After they'd gone, Natasha automatically began to tidy up—but as she straightened from stacking some magazines neatly in the rack she caught sight of herself in the mirror, and was momentarily transfixed by the image which gazed back at her. Anna was right. Her face was pale and her eyes were like huge, dark saucers—dominating her face with a look of restless uncertainty.

The front door slammed, and Natasha hastily turned away from the mirror as Raffaele walked slowly back into the room, loosening his tie, an inexplicable look in his eyes. She was reminded, all too vividly, of the sweet sensation of his kiss, the sensational feel of his hands on her breasts.

'What's the matter, Natasha?' he mocked. 'You don't look very happy.'

'Was that display really necessary?' she questioned.

'And what display would that be?' he questioned, flinging his tie onto the table.

'All that touchy-feely stuff in front of Anna,' she retorted, resisting the urge to pick up the tie and fold it for him, picking up the babysitter's used coffee mug instead.

He shrugged, his eyes dancing as he recognised the tell-tale signs of sexual frustration in her expression, the angry little way she was wriggling her hips. 'But we're engaged to be married, *cara,*' he protested innocently, and drifted his eyes over the pinpoint thrust of her nipples against the slippery scarlet satin of her gown. 'Or had you forgotten? Bedtime, I think—don't you? Oh, and don't forget to turn the lights out, will you?' he added deliberately, and then he was gone.

Natasha was left staring at the empty space in the door, feeling as though some psychological battle had just been fought.

And Raffaele had won.

# CHAPTER EIGHT

NATASHA didn't see the newspapers until after she took Sam to school next morning. She had overslept, and only just remembered to put on her engagement ring after throwing on yet more new clothes.

She woke her son and went downstairs to make coffee and toast, with the massive diamond winking and flashing on her finger like a star. Would anyone at the school notice? she wondered, but doubted it. Early on at the school she had been assessed by the super-rich mums and accorded her own particular status—which was why she mainly mixed with the au pairs.

She did her best not to react when Raffaele walked into the kitchen, waving his one free hand around in the air as he spoke in animated and exasperated French into a mobile phone. But it wasn't easy. She wondered if that little scene in the back of the car had given him the same concern which had left her staring at the bedroom ceiling for most of the night.

'He's talking to a bank in Paris,' translated Sam as he carefully poured honey over his porridge. 'An' he's *very* cross.'

Natasha thought that you wouldn't need Sam's superiority with languages to be able to work *that* out! Though, to be honest, Raffaele might as well have been singing in Swahili for all the notice she would have taken of what he was saying. She was too busy trying not to ogle him.

He was wearing a city suit, but even the formal design of the outfit was unable to detract from his raw sexuality and masculinity. His black hair was faintly ruffled and he looked the picture of glowing vitality.

Natasha held up the *cafetière*, the way she always did, and Raffaele nodded his head vigorously—just the way *he* always did. Or did she imagine a faint quirk of his lips and that slight narrowing of his eyes? Even if it *was* simply her imagination her memory came thudding in to add to her discomfiture. Natasha was very aware that her hand was shaking, and she slopped some coffee into the saucer.

Raffaele raised his brows fractionally, his eyes

dancing dark mischief as he clicked off his phone and shook his head when she offered him toast.

'*No, grazie,*' he murmured. 'Strangely enough, I have little appetite for food this morning. Why, Natasha—you've spilt the coffee! You seem a little on edge—is something troubling you?'

Yes, she wanted to shout. *You* are! But, of course, she couldn't do that because Sam was sitting in the room—and there would be no explanation in the world you could give to a five-year-old to explain why you had started shouting at your boss and behaving so uncharacteristically.

And then—to Natasha's fury—the two of them began to chat to each other in Italian—making her feel completely redundant. She really was going to have to work a bit harder at the language—she hadn't really progressed much beyond the days of the week and being able to ask for directions to the railway station.

'Have you nearly finished, Sam?' she asked pointedly as the minutes ticked by. 'Yes? Then run up and brush your teeth and we'll go.'

'Yes, Mama.'

Sam jumped up, grinned at Raffaele, and ran out of the room. Natasha grabbed an apple from out of the fruit bowl and made to follow him.

'Oh, Natasha?'

Keep it neutral, she told herself. 'Yes?'

'You're in the papers. Or should I say *we're* in the papers.'

Heart pounding, she stared at him. 'Have you seen them?'

He gave a short laugh. 'You know I don't bother reading the tabloids.'

'How do you know, then?'

'Troy rang me first thing. He seems pleased with the results.' The expression on his face told her nothing about his own feelings on the matter. 'You can buy them on your way back from school, if you're interested.'

'Of course I'm interested!' She turned her head and noticed for the first time the faint blue shadows underneath his eyes. 'Aren't you even a little bit curious about what they say?'

'What they *say* is largely irrelevant—getting the item in the papers was the main purpose of this exercise, remember?' he questioned coolly.

Was that designed to put her in her place? To remind her that they might have shared kisses and intimate embraces but that she remained the woman who served him his coffee and offered him his toast.

'Of course I remember,' she said lightly. They

stared at one another across the of the wide expanse of the basement kitchen, with its huge range and its copper pots and the exquisite antique tiles which had been imported at great expense from Italy. A bowl of fruit lay in the centre of a scrubbed wooden table which stood on the beautiful worn stone floor tiles.

It looked like one of those illustrations from a magazine—everyone's dream kitchen. Natasha had heard some of his friends expressing surprise when they saw it for the first time, especially the girlfriends. Perhaps they expected something streamlined and slickly modern, instead of the traditional. But Natasha had recognised early on that there was a side of Raffaele which was fiercely traditional.

It was why she had dared to make the odd little addition to the room—the slim coloured glass bottles lined up on the windowsill which she'd discovered as a bargain in a junk shop, the small jug of flowers on the dresser.

But this morning the familiar terrain of the kitchen seemed different—or maybe it *felt* different, just as Natasha did. It seemed that it was impossible for a man to awaken your senses and for you to carry on treating that man exactly the same as you'd done before.

She kept wavering between wanting to put as much space between them as possible and wanting to run into his arms, to have him hold her tightly and to kiss her again in that almost unbearably sweet way. He had made her feel like a woman—a real flesh-and-blood creature—with desires she had hidden away for so long she'd almost forgotten they existed.

She turned away before he could see her sudden rise in colour and guess its cause.

'Oh—and just one more thing, Natasha.'

She swallowed down the erotic memory. 'Yes?'

'I've been invited to a cocktail party at the Italian Embassy on Wednesday. You will, of course, accompany me.'

'Of course.'

'And next weekend I have a business meeting which will spill over into the social.' His voice dipped. 'Is your passport up to date?'

Her embarrassment forgotten, she turned back to face him. 'Why?'

'Because, *mia cara,* the meeting will most probably be abroad.'

She shook her head. 'Well, I can't do that.'

'Oh?' Raffaele's eyes narrowed. 'Why not?'

Was he being completely dense? 'Because of Sam, of course.'

'Because of *what* about Sam, *mia bella?*'

'I can't leave him for a whole weekend to go *abroad!* Why, I've only ever even left him for a single night before. You know that.'

'*Si*, I know that,' he said, and his black gaze locked on hers with piercing thoughtfulness. 'And maybe it is something you ought to think about.'

She certainly wasn't imagining the reproachful note in his voice, or that faint flicker of censure in his eyes. 'You make that sound like a criticism,' she said shakily, knowing that she could stand almost anything but that. Because in a way her whole life was centred around Sam's needs—and any disapproval of that would surely throw into question her whole existence.

'It was not intended to be quite that.' He paused, spread his hands in that typically continental gesture he sometimes used. 'But it might do you both good to have a break from each other.'

'You're saying we have a claustrophobic relationship?' she demanded.

'I can see I've touched a raw nerve,' he said acidly.

'Maybe you just can't stand the fact that someone else's needs might come before *your* wishes.'

She was clearly spoiling for a fight, and Raffaele almost gave a low, cynical laugh. Almost. But he recognised that this wasn't getting them anywhere. There was a reason why they were both so tetchy—and it was the same reason why sleep had refused to come last night. It was the needs of their hungry bodies, demanding to be fed—and so they would be.

'It is pointless arguing about it, since I will need you with me,' he stated tersely. 'Arrange for Sam to go to a friend's—it will be fun for him, and good for you to have a break. What about Serge—they get on well, don't they?'

Natasha nodded. She hadn't been aware that he'd noticed—but, as usual, he had a point. And Sam *did* love Serge. Natasha was sure the French boy's parents would be only too pleased to have her son for a few nights.

But a weekend away in the company of others with the man she was pretending to be marrying threw up a whole new set of problems. She put the apple in her handbag. 'Won't we be expected to share a room?' she said slowly.

He studied her. 'Oh, Natasha—come on!' he remonstrated softly. 'What do you think? Unless they're having a Return to Chastity

Weekend most modern engaged couples *do* have sex and *do* share rooms.' His eyes fired her a challenge, but deep down he felt the aching insistence of desire. 'And do not look so shocked, *cara*. Not to put too fine a point on it—you and I were well on the way to having sex in the back of the car last night!'

She stared at him, her heart thundering in her chest. 'How *dare* you say something like that?' she hissed.

He raised his eyebrows in mock-surprise but, oh, he was enjoying this. Whoever would have thought that Natasha kept such fire hidden beneath her mousy little exterior? 'Keep your voice down—or don't you mind Sam hearing you chastising me?'

She shook her head distractedly. What was he *doing?* He seemed to have her tied up in twists and knots and circles, and she should be hating him, resenting him—when all the time, she…she…

'No,' he murmured, as he watched her, 'it would be the best solution, I agree, but, unfortunately, I can't come over there and kiss you, Natasha—no matter how much you want me to.'

He met her indignant gaze and let his own travel with arrogant amusement over her flushed cheeks, and down farther still—to where her breasts peaked against the soft cashmere of her sweater. 'Go on,' he taunted. 'I dare you to deny it with any conviction! You can't, can you?'

'I'm going to take Sam to school!' she declared, and grabbed her bag.

'Running away?' he mocked.

'Running to sanity!' she retorted.

'Well, make sure you're free that weekend,' he said softly.

It sounded more like an ultimatum than a request, and the accompanying look which he sent lancing towards her made little goose-bumps ice their way all over her skin.

Natasha tried to concentrate on Sam's chatter as they searched the pavement for conkers, the way they always did, but all she could think about was Raffaele. Matters weren't helped when she approached the wrought iron gates of the school and sensed, rather than saw, people turning to stare at her.

Usually she felt pretty much invisible—but there was no doubt that her makeover had turned her into a much more acceptable version of a woman. Blondes fared better than mouse—Marilyn Monroe had discovered that decades ago.

This morning she had dressed down, and wasn't looking radically different from usual, even though the jacket she wore was softly luxurious—but people were definitely noticing the ring. That's why Raffaele bought it, she reminded herself, with a stab of something which felt unreasonably like disappointment.

She kissed Sam goodbye and watched him running across the playground. Then she saw one of the other mothers approaching, with an expression of grim determination on her face. This was a woman who had barely deigned to glance at her before today—a woman who was clearly very good friends with her plastic surgeon.

'Hello—*Natasha,* isn't it?'

Natasha nodded, and pulled her new jacket closer. 'Hello. Yes, that's right. I'm afraid I don't know your—'

But the woman was in no mood for introductions. 'Someone said that you and Raffaele de Feretti were…' Her disbelieving tone faded away the moment her sharp eyes alighted on Natasha's hand, and she snatched it up as if she had every right to. 'So it's *true!*'

Her hostile and disbelieving tone made the lie easier—you're doing this for Elisabetta, Natasha reminded herself. 'Yes, it's true,' she agreed pleasantly. 'It's all been a bit of a whirlwind!'

'But…'

Natasha raised her eyebrows in question. 'Yes?'

'Aren't you his *housekeeper?*'

Natasha's heart was thudding like a piston, but somehow she kept her face calm. 'Actually, I prefer to describe myself as his *fiancée,*' she said, with a glow which felt dangerously like triumph.

But that was the wrong emotion to be feeling, she told herself as she hurried away in a sudden bluster of dark falling leaves. She had nothing to be triumphant about because none of this was real. She was simply playing a game, and even if her motives for doing it were sound she had to remember not to get sucked into the fairytale. Particularly when the fiction of being betrothed to a man you'd always secretly desired was so overwhelming. Yes, she wanted him—but what woman wouldn't?

Raffaele wanted her, too—he had made that very plain. He had wanted her in the highly charged atmosphere of the car last night, but she had seen the gleam of desire in the seemingly innocent surroundings of the kitchen this morning, as well. And, in a way, that had been infinitely more dangerous. It was easy to yearn for someone when you'd been drinking champagne all evening and were all dressed up—but to feel the same way in the cold, clear light of day... Well, that could easily send out the wrong message to someone like her.

Because lust meant nothing—it was just a part of Raffaele's restless and seeking nature. His power and his alpha-maleness would put sex high on his list of priorities—for him, it would come as naturally as breathing. And Natasha would get hurt if she wasn't careful. Not just because she was a woman and she placed different values on sex, but because of the way she felt about him.

The little newsagents was tucked away just off the busy main road—it was such an old-fashioned shop that Natasha used to wonder how long it would be able to survive in the face of the supermarket giants who were sweeping small businesses away.

On tall shelves were jars of brightly coloured sweets, and from the ceiling bobbed a few bats, while chocolates, foil-wrapped to look like pumpkins, lay on the counter—for Halloween was fast approaching.

'Getting blustery out there,' said the owner,

an old man who wore fingerless gloves and still liked to add up in his head. 'It'll be winter soon.'

'Oh, don't say that!' Natasha protested.

She bought stamps and two tabloids, but she didn't open them until she was almost home. *But it's not really your home,* mocked a voice in her head as she let herself into the garden square. *It's Raffaele's home, not yours.* As the wind flapped the pages of the newspapers, she wondered if it was the 'engagement' which had suddenly made her start thinking like this, and a shiver ran over her skin as she realised that what she had agreed to had changed everything.

*That nothing was ever going to be the same again.*

She leafed through the first paper and there it was—the shot taken when they'd arrived at the charity ball and first stepped onto the red carpet to face a battery of cameras.

Raffaele had cupped her elbow and bent his head close to hers, asking her if she was okay— his look one of solicitude rather than passion. In a society of easy sex and quick kicks it was the image of caring which had convinced the hacks that Raffaele de Feretti's heart had finally melted.

They said that the camera never lied, but it wasn't quite as simple as that. It picked up on what it saw—and then interpreted it to fit its own agenda. The image selected showed the one true emotion expressed in a whole evening of pretending. Raffaele's concern for her had been genuine, the emotion had been genuine—and that was what had convinced the gossip columnists that this was, indeed, *the real thing!*

Natasha's fingers were trembling as she read it.

After dating some of the wealthiest and most beautiful heiresses in Europe, Italian billionaire playboy Raffaele de Feretti has astonished everyone by becoming engaged to his housekeeper, Natasha Phillips. Ms Phillips, 25, who is a single parent, was photographed showing off her ring—a giant two-carat solitaire—at a charity ball last night. If diamonds are a girl's best friend, then lucky Natasha has one hell of a buddy!

How peculiar it was to read about yourself in the third person like this, she thought—and even more peculiar was the sight of *her* photo featured in a national newspaper. It didn't look like her at all—with her coiled and elaborate hair and her shimmery silk-satin evening gown. She looked like an expensive stranger.

Yet if she examined it more closely she could see her expression as she reassured Raffaele that she was okay. Would anyone else notice the soft look of adoration which was sparking from her eyes as she looked at him? If he gave the picture more than a cursory glance would he guess at her secret, or just think that she was a fine actress?

She walked home slowly, thinking of what Raffaele had said about her rarely being parted from her son. His words had implied that this was a failing rather than a strength, and for the first time Natasha began to wonder if perhaps she used Sam as an excuse not to go out there and live life properly. Did she? Was he one of those children doomed to be tied to his mother's apron strings? And was she in danger of becoming the kind of woman who resented her child growing up and growing away?

Galvanised into action, she telephoned Serge's parents and asked if Sam could go and stay the following weekend. They were delighted to oblige.

'*Mais, oui—bien sûr!*' Serge's mother laughed. 'You wish to have some time alone with your husband-to-be, *oui?*'

That rubbed at Natasha's conscience—but

Elisabetta's pinched and wan face swam into her memory. 'If that's okay?' she said.

'It is more than okay. Go and have a wonderful time,' whispered Madame Bertrand.

Natasha didn't even want to think about it and, instead, began to sort out the walk-in larder. It was deeply satisfying to create order out of chaos, and it also served as a kind of distraction therapy.

The ring felt odd and scratchy as she dipped it in and out of a bucket of hot and soapy water, so she slid on a pair of rubber gloves and smiled. If only the *Daily View* could see her now—how different she looked to the image of herself which was plastered over page five of the paper! But she needed to do this. *Because this is my reality,* she reminded herself. *After all this is over I'll have to go back to a normal existence—where I won't be whisked in chauffeur-driven cars to charity balls. Or kissed by black-eyed Italians who can make you feel as if you've found heaven in their arms.*

The telephone rang, and she peeled the gloves off and went to answer it.

'Natasha?'

The rich, accented voice spilled over her senses like honey. 'Yes, Raffaele?'

There was a pause. 'On your recent shopping trip, did you by any chance buy some swimwear?'

'Sw-swimwear?' Had he meant the word to sound X-rated, or was it simply what it implied—heat and sun and partially clothed bodies? Natasha closed her eyes as she recalled the teeny bikini which the personal shopper had told her would be a sin not to buy. And the halter-neck one-piece in acid-green which made her body look as curvy as a coiled snake.

'It's a simple question,' he said impatiently. 'And I'm about to go into a meeting! Yes or no?'

'I did.' She swallowed. 'Why?'

From the penthouse suite which housed his office, Raffaele looked out over the skyscrapers of the city and gave a grim smile of satisfaction.

'Then you'd better pack it. You remember I told you to keep next weekend free?' There was a pause. 'We are going to Marrakech, *cara*.'

# CHAPTER NINE

'You do realise—' Raffaele paused deliberately as he watched her reach up, the silk of her robe brushing against her waist as she did so, and he found himself marvelling at how such a simple movement could be so damned provocative. He flicked his tongue over lips which were suddenly bone-dry. 'That I need to know a few details about your life.'

Natasha turned round. She had been hanging up clothes in the sumptuous bedroom and trying not to act too dazed by the level of luxury she had been subjected to ever since their private jet had landed in Morocco. But it hadn't been easy. This was opulence on a scale she hadn't realised existed.

A car had been waiting to whisk them to the ancient city of Marrakech, surrounded by the famous rose-pink walls, its streets lined with fragrant orange trees, with old-fashioned pony and traps trotting along amid the spluttering cars.

It was hard for Natasha to believe that a place could be so gloriously hot in October and the sky such a clear, bright blue, and she breathed in the scented air with a kind of startled delight after the misty cool of autumnal England. She had never been abroad anywhere before—something which Raffaele had found hard to believe—and this would have been a wonderful place to start if it hadn't been for her worries about sharing a suite with him.

The opulent *riad* in which they were to stay was situated right in the very heart of Marrakech. It was an oasis of comfort and luxury, with a massage room and sauna as well as large, opulent suites—pure, decadent comfort, and situated only minutes from the bustling Medina, with its narrow alleyways and exotic goods and general air of mystery.

It was also, as Raffaele had pointed out, accessible by car—both a luxury and a rarity in the region. Revelation seemed to follow on from revelation and he had saved the most astonishing fact until last—much to Natasha's amazement—they were to be the guests of a sheikh.

'A *real* sheikh?' she breathed.

'I think that Zahid would be outraged to be described as a fake,' came his laconic reply.

'Would you mind telling me why we're spending the weekend with a sheikh—how you even *know* one?'

Raffaele smiled. 'He's someone I do business with. Someone I happen to like. And he will expect me to bring a woman with me.'

*Who would Raffaele have brought if he weren't pretending to be in a relationship with me?* wondered Natasha, unprepared for the swift, sharp tang of jealousy—but somehow she kept it from showing on her face. She was getting rather good at concealing her emotions.

'Doesn't he have a palace?' she queried instead.

'Of course he does. He has several, *cara mia*. But he, too, will be accompanied by a woman. Like you, she is a Westerner—and that is frowned upon by his people. So he takes his consorts elsewhere.'

Natasha found herself wondering what this 'consort' thought of being hidden away like a guilty secret. But that was none of her business.

'And, anyway,' Raffaele murmured, 'that is enough about Zahid. I told you—I want to learn about *you, mia bella*.'

Natasha shook her head in disbelief. 'But

I've been living in your house for over three years,' she objected. 'Surely, you know *something* about me?'

He could see the faint puzzlement and hurt which had momentarily crumpled her rose-petal lips, and he hardened his heart against it. It wasn't her place to be offended—to look at him with those big blue eyes. Did she imagine that it was some kind of interest in her as a person which made him ask, instead of plain necessity?

The sight of the enormous bed seemed to tantalise him with its allure, and to make him examine his own motives—it had since they'd arrived. Was he going to seduce her? And if so—when? Perhaps that was the real reason behind his question—a kind of distraction while he made his mind up? To see whether she would be suitable to seduce—or whether she would be foolish enough to read more into it than was there.

'On the contrary,' he demurred. 'I need a little of the kind of detail which a man in love would be expected to know.'

*A man in love.* It didn't mean anything, but that didn't stop her stupid heart reacting, even while she realised that this was simply Raffaele through and through. He excelled at everything he did—and he wanted to excel at being a fiancé! It would be intolerable for him to be found out—for other people to discover that the whole situation was a sham—and that was what had prompted him into asking her. Or did she imagine that a little heavy petting in the back of a limousine would be enough to win the affection of a sophisticated man-of-the-world like him?

'What exactly do you want to know?' she asked.

'Your childhood. Schooling. That kind of thing. A whole life to get through.' Shrugging his broad shoulders, he wandered over to one of the cushioned divans which overlooked the central courtyard and slid down on it, black eyes like chips of jet. 'Why, if you manage to keep it brief, we might even be able to cover your likes and dislikes before we get called for dinner!'

Natasha glared at him. Had the put-down been deliberate? Did he just want to get it over with as quickly as possible because she was boring? Well, *damn* him!

'I was brought up by a maiden aunt—'

'Your parents?' he intercepted swiftly.

For a moment, she was tempted to tell him that if he kept interrupting they would never be able to 'keep it brief,' but some instinct of self-preservation told her not to bring discord into the bedroom.

'My parents both died within a couple of years of one another. My aunt was older.'

'And strict?'

She sighed. 'Raffaele, is all this necessary? I thought we had a whole life to get through.'

Something in her gentle admonishment made him wince, and yet something else disturbed him far more. The fact that he *wanted to know!* And why was that? Because for the first time in his life he had met a woman who wasn't gushing to tell him everything bar her inside leg measurement?

'I want to know,' he said stubbornly.

And, of course, what Raffaele wanted he always got—didn't he? 'Yes, she was strict,' said Natasha, and then to stop him from reaching the obvious conclusion for himself, and thinking that he was some kind of psychological genius, she elaborated. 'In fact, she was so strict that I'd barely been allowed any kind of social life before I went to university.' She met the look in his eyes and nodded. 'That was where it all went wrong. Freedom came as a bit of a double-edged sword, really—I wanted it, but I was scared of it, too. And, of course. I didn't have any real experiences of going out, drinking, dancing. The sort of things that most people my age had grown up with.'

He suddenly caught a glimpse of the girl she must have been then—with the unworldly air which had remained pretty much intact until her recent makeover. 'And what about Sam's father?'

Well, she might be able to see the purpose of allowing him a recap of her past life, but he certainly didn't need to know the fine details of *that*. Sam's father had just been looking for thrills—not a lifelong commitment. And in a way Natasha hadn't been able to blame him—because she hadn't been looking to have a baby, either. But accidents happened—and just because Sam hadn't been planned it didn't mean that he didn't have every right to be loved and nurtured and cherished.

'Sam's father has many attributes,' she said carefully.

'Why doesn't he see his boy?'

Natasha frowned. 'Does it matter?'

'I want to know.' He met the challenge in her eyes. 'For research purposes, you understand,' he elaborated coolly.

'He wanted nothing to do with the pregnancy,' she said flatly. 'He has never even seen his child, and nor has he wanted to.'

He saw the fierce expression of pride masking the hurt on her face and something turned over inside him. 'Natasha—'

She shook her head, shaking away his meaningless expression of sympathy. She didn't *need* that. 'But *I* wanted the baby—no matter how he was created. And, in many ways, it's easier this way. At least I've been spared the emotional warfare which comes when two parents are separated. Sam has never known anything but love and I've never regretted my decision—not for a single second!'

In a way he applauded her fiery spirit, yet also he cursed her—because nothing drew a man to a woman more than a flame. Didn't she realise that he wanted her in his arms, that he desired her intensely and that something seemed to be blocking his desire every step of the way?

First, he had hesitated because of the inequality of their social standing. Yet now her feisty defiance in the face of what must have been a difficult time seemed to be blocking him, yet again. So what was stopping him?

Was it his *conscience?*

Raffaele frowned. He must stop being sentimental—because nobody could accuse *her* of that. She had coolly stated that it suited her for Sam's father not to be around, just as she had coolly agreed to masquerade as *his* fiancé. She was a pragmatic woman who had demonstrated that she had a woman's needs—needs which she'd admirably suppressed during Sam's early years.

But Sam wasn't around now. For once, she was free of responsibility. They were both adults who wanted one another—didn't they deserve a little light relief in the form of a mutually explosive passion?

He studied her. Her hair was a silken tumble around her shoulders and the long gauzy dress she had sensibly worn in such a strict country hinted distractingly at the lush firm body which lay beneath. Her painted toenails peeped out from the front of woven leather sandals, quietly informing him that her long legs were bare, and suddenly he ached to have them wrapped around his naked back. But she was surveying him as warily as a cornered animal, and Raffaele—who was a master of timing—recognised that the time was not right.

He rose from the divan with all the languid

grace of some jungle cat and picked up an air-light linen jacket.

'I'm going to have my meeting with Zahid before dinner—you might wish to freshen up,' he drawled, and his eyes met hers as he wished that he could stay and watch her.

Natasha found her cheeks colouring as she watched him go, wondering if there was some kind of acceptable behaviour for sharing a suite with a man. Rules which most normal people were aware of but which had passed her by. Was there some kind of code you used when you needed to go to the bathroom?

She waited until she was sure he had gone, and then gathered together all her fresh clothes and lingerie—terrified of having to emerge from her shower looking in any way vulnerable in case Raffaele should suddenly appear. Because, in a way, all this watchful waiting was playing havoc with her senses.

She knew he wanted her—despite her laughable lack of experience with the opposite sex. Even if it wasn't for the telltale glint she sometimes saw in the depths of those ebony eyes, a man like Raffaele could not disguise the sexuality which seemed to exude from every pore of his remarkable body.

The trouble was that she wanted him, too.

So where did that leave her? Wondering and worrying about whether to go through with her heart's greatest wish—or protecting that self-same heart by denying it?

The bathroom increased her trepidation even while it appealed to her senses—it was all marble and mosaic and mirrors. Costly essences lined a spa bath so wide and deep that you could almost imagine floating in it, and someone had placed bowls of fresh crimson rose petals on the pristine white surfaces.

But Natasha had spent too much of her adult life catering to other people's needs not to allow herself to enjoy this. Freedom and luxury—what a pleasure. Closing her eyes, she slicked on the creamy soap, creating layers of foamy suds over her breasts…breasts which were growing unusually heavy…

The minutes melted by as the memory of Raffaele's kiss swam into her head with erotic clarity. Her body stirred restlessly beneath the scented water, and in the end Natasha got out. Heading for the shower, she turned the temperature right down until she was so cold that she was shivering as she wrapped herself in an oversized white towelling robe to dry.

She slithered into the brand-new lingerie and a long, silky robe, and when she'd dried her hair and put on a little make-up she stepped back to inspect herself in the full-length mirror.

The woman who stared back at her might have blended in perfectly with the luxurious surroundings, but it certainly didn't look like the Natasha *she* knew. It didn't *feel* like Natasha, either. The new bra and panties fitted as comfortably as a second skin, but they were making her uncomfortably aware of her body. Of the strange new dull ache which seemed to tingle at her skin just lately. But she would be a hypocrite if she pretended to try and pinpoint when that longing had begun, because it was engraved on her memory as well as her heart.

*Ever since the afternoon when Raffaele had kissed her!*

Drawing a deep breath for courage, and telling herself that to embroil herself any deeper than she already was would be sheer madness, Natasha pushed the door open and walked into the suite.

He was waiting for her. Reclining on a heap of lavish velvet and brocade cushions, looking such a mass of contradictions. Sexy and passionate—yet cool and calculating. His olive skin glowed softly, like deep golden silk. And those legs. Natasha swallowed. So impossibly long. His whole pose was both languid and watchful, and she found herself wondering how he managed to be all those things at once.

'I note that you have learnt to make a man wait, *mia cara,*' he murmured approvingly.

She swallowed, wishing that the huge room didn't suddenly feel as though it had telescoped into matchbox proportions. 'I'm not playing games with you, Raffaele.'

'Well, you should,' he reprimanded softly. 'Games are good, because men like to believe they are being played with.'

'D-did you have your meeting with the Sheikh?'

'I did.'

Edgily, her fingers pleated at the soft silk which covered her thigh. 'What was it about?'

'You want to hear the details about the new conference centre which is being built in Zahid's country?'

'No. Not really.' Natasha turned away from the mocking distraction of his ebony eyes. 'What time's dinner?' she asked, a note of slight desperation in her voice.

'Not until seven.'

'Oh!' Another hour to kill. Sixty long

minutes in such gloriously tempting confinement with him. How the hell was she going to get through it?

'Natasha?'

His deep voice broke into her thoughts.

'Natasha, look at me.'

Reluctantly, she turned back and did as he asked, afraid of what she would read in his face—what kind of new temptation she would find there. 'What?' she whispered.

'You look very beautiful tonight, in your robe of silk and with your hair like coils of satin. Do you know that?'

She wanted to tell *him* not to play games. Not to seduce her with his honeyed words and that look of approbation which seemed to wash sweetly over her skin. Not to tell her she was beautiful when she knew deep down that she was plain and ordinary Natasha Phillips, who just happened to have had a lot of money and care thrown her way.

But the oddest thing of all was that he made her *feel* beautiful. As if it wasn't a game at all. As if the words he spoke were true. As if he were saying them to someone for the very first time.

And how crazy was that?

With his long list of lovers, Raffaele must

have told a woman she was beautiful almost as often as he'd made yet another major takeover!

Snapping herself out of the spell he seemed to have woven around her, Natasha forced a smile. 'Do you happen to know your way around this vast place?' she asked.

'No.' A spark of interest flared from the black eyes. 'But I have a pretty good sense of direction.'

'Shall we have a guided tour of the *riad* before dinner, then?' she questioned guilelessly.

Reluctantly, he applauded her manipulation, acknowledging that the air had been becoming fraught with tension and knowing that it might have built up to such an extent that there would have been no alternative but to kiss her.

*But you are planning to kiss her, anyway.*

'What a wonderful idea,' he said softly, his eyes a dark gleam. 'Let's go.'

She followed him downstairs to the cool, central courtyard she'd seen briefly when they'd arrived and which dominated the ground floor. It was almost as if they were walking on a cool carpet of different kinds of marble—in colours ranging from palest cream to a rich sand and every shade in between.

Tall candles were being blown gently by the lightest of breezes, and by now a soft dusk had begun to fall. The warm air was scented with some heady fragrance which Natasha didn't recognise, and her senses felt as if they were slowly coming to life.

The courtyard led onto a large swimming pool, its turquoise waters illuminated from within, and Natasha gasped.

'Oh, but that's beautiful!' she exclaimed.

'You can swim?' Raffaele asked.

'Of course.'

'We could steal down here later, when the house is asleep,' he suggested, and saw the way she bit her lip. 'You could show me what a nymph you are in the water.'

Abruptly, Natasha turned and began walking away, her heart thundering, wanting to tell him not to make suggestions like that, but afraid that he would hear the longing in her voice if she attempted to carry through such a blatant lie.

His footfall was soft, but he was following her, and she barely knew where she was going other than around a maze of corridors—some light, some dark—as if she was taking part in some bizarre game of hide and seek. Or as if he was the hunter and she the quarry. A quarry that had no desire to escape.

Raffaele knew what she was doing. The

language of her body was calling out to him like a siren, but he recognised that she did not want to be seen to be complicit in her own desires. She wanted him to take her, as women had longed to be taken since the beginning of time.

He felt his mouth dry as he quickened his pace and watched hers slow. So easy to reach her. So ridiculously easy. He reached for her, capturing her waist with his hands, and turned her around, seeing the way her eyes darkened and her lips parted as she gazed up at him.

'Natasha,' he ground out, in a voice which was harsh with desire.

Thoughts flew into her mind. That she could stop him. That she *should* stop him. That this was leading absolutely nowhere other than to certain heartbreak. But wasn't this a dream which Natasha had cherished and nurtured, despite trying not to? Like a tiny seed which someone had planted in a dark cupboard she hadn't been able to help herself from feeding it, occasionally allowing light in on it, so that it had just grown and grown.

'Raffaele,' she said unsteadily, and just the saying of his name was like granting herself a forbidden luxury. Like the turning of a key in a door which had always been locked.

And suddenly his lips were on hers, and Natasha was letting him kiss her, not fighting him—not in any way. She had wanted this for much too long to deny it any longer. Moaning at the first sweet taste of his mouth, she felt the hot chase of her breathing and the eager surrender of her body as he pulled her into a darkened alcove.

# CHAPTER TEN

His lips were hot and hungry, his body hard.

'Raffaele!' Natasha moaned against his mouth, gripping at his broad shoulders for fear that she should sway and fall.

'You want this,' he said unsteadily, not asking but stating.

Some last vestige of sanity swam into her mind. 'The servants—'

'There are no servants, *cara,*' he ground out. 'In a place like this they are taught to look the other way.'

Natasha stiffened. Was that how he saw *her,* back in London? Cooking breakfast for the women who had shared his bed and then slipping into the shadows when her presence was no longer required?

The sentiment unsettled her—but not enough to stop her. Not enough to make her hold back from reaching up to grip those muscular broad shoulders, or from sighing out her pleasure as he pulled her closer.

It was as if she had been made to be held by him. To be wrapped in his arms with his heart beating against her breast. She closed her eyes as he slid his palms proprietorially over each of her silk-covered buttocks, letting her feel the hard cradle of his desire.

'Raffaele,' she breathed shakily.

'Our bodies match, *si?*' he murmured. 'They fit together perfectly.'

'Like a jigsaw,' she whispered, barely realising that she had said it aloud until she heard his low laugh of pleasure.

'But a jigsaw with one vital piece missing, I think.'

His voice sounded suddenly different. Deepened with desire and a sense of purpose. But Natasha had no time to be nervous, because now one hard, muscular thigh was parting hers—though it only seemed to increase the terrible growing ache within her rather than relieving it.

'You like that?' he questioned, as his mouth whispered over the base of her throat.

She swallowed. *'Yes!'*

Raffaele reached round to take one soft breast

in his hand, his thumb beginning to tease the hard thrust of her nipple as it peaked through the light material of the dress, and he felt the shudder of pleasure which rippled through her body. 'This, too?'

She closed her eyes. *'Yes!'* She knew where this was heading, where she wanted it to go. Something in Raffaele's touch incited her as well as excited her—and she was suddenly filled with the urgent desire to touch him back. To dare to feel him as he was feeling her. She drifted her hands down, over his chest, over the taut board of his torso. He groaned his approval.

*'Ancora di piu.* More!' he translated huskily, and then groaned again as he felt her fingers tiptoe farther down, seeming to hesitate before cupping him, as if testing the weight there, as if she were intimately assessing his body. And it was a situation so bizarre that Natasha should be doing this—should be touching him in such a way which was making him harder than he could ever remember being before—that he very nearly exploded there and then, in that dark and scented alcove.

He bent his mouth to her ear, to the perfumed bright hair. Where had his little mouse gone now? 'Take off your panties,' he murmured.

Distractedly, she shook her head.

'No?'

'It's…'

'It's, what?' he prompted on a throaty murmur.

'It's *wrong*… We…we…*shouldn't*.'

'Shouldn't we?'

'N-no!'

But her actions were belying her words and, unseen, he smiled as he reached down to ruck up the filmy fabric of her gown, sliding his hand up the cool silk of her inner thigh with delicate yet ruthless efficiency. Like a dance he had engaged in so many times before, the moves were as natural to him as breathing. And so was her reaction. The shudder. The little cry as his fingertip alighted on that most vulnerable and feminine part of her. But the sense of wonder which made her voice shiver into that incredulous little gasp— surely that was Natasha's and Natasha's alone?

'Are you quite sure we shouldn't?' he urged, as he moved his provocative finger away and heard her muffled and slurred little sound of objection.

'No… I mean, yes… I mean…'

But Raffaele knew exactly what she meant, and he began to tug at the moist little scrap of material with a low growl, his own erection so hard that it was actually painful.

At that moment a low bell began to ring.

They both froze, and Natasha was the first one to act—trying to pull away from him. But he held her firm.

'Let me *go!*'

He could smell the heady incense of her desire and grazed his lips to her earlobe. 'Let me take you first.'

Wasn't it appalling that part of her should thrill to that outrageous demand—or was it only natural when he murmured in that silken, accented voice? And maybe she should be grateful that he'd said it—because although Natasha was terribly aroused, aching for him, the sexist and matter-of-fact way he had stated his intention brought her to her senses.

Or rather, *away* from her senses.

This time, fired by indignation and given strength by just how dreadful it would look should someone stumble upon them, she managed to extricate herself from the enticement of his embrace.

'Raffaele! We must stop it,' she urged furiously, and she began to tug her clothing straight and lift her fingertips to her hot and flushed cheeks in a vain effort to cool them.

Through the dim light he raised his eyebrows imperiously. 'Why?'

'Why do you think? Because our host happens to be summoning us to dinner and is waiting for us!'

He shrugged. 'Zahid will understand.'

For some reason his careless excuse offended her even more. 'Well, maybe he will,' she stormed softly. 'But it would be an unforgivable breach of good manners, and one that *I* certainly wouldn't tolerate.'

He stared at her, seeing the situation through her eyes for the first time and suddenly he understood. She wasn't just thinking of her own reputation—and he had to admit he hadn't really been thinking about it either, had he? She was concerned about all the people who would be waiting to serve them with what would undoubtedly be a lavish dinner.

Raffaele was used to people waiting for *him,* but for Natasha it was the exact opposite. She was always at his beck and call, wasn't she? Waiting on his wishes and his commands. But this weekend was different. He had asked her to masquerade as someone else, and she was obeying him to the letter!

Somewhere along the way she seemed to have acquired all the haughty attributes which actually made her believable as his fiancée. She was telling him what to do—and he could tell by the expression on his face that he would not be able to change her mind. At least, not now.

He nodded curtly as they stepped out into the courtyard once more, but frustration continued to linger in his blood—and something about the way she had admonished him perturbed him.

Because he had thought of them as not being equals—yet hadn't Natasha just demonstrated the exact opposite by her actions? When had a woman last told Raffaele what to do? Never in his adult life, that was for sure. And when had a woman last stopped him from making love to her?

Never.

The bell rang again, and they turned in its direction. But just before they set off he caught her by the arm—and heard her sharp intake of breath, saw the way her eyes darkened at just that light touch.

'Very well,' he whispered, recognising the power he had over her with silent satisfaction. 'We will go in to dinner and we will play the attentive guests—but never doubt for one moment what I intend for us to do later, once we can excuse ourselves. I shall spend the evening feasting on the sight of your kiss-bruised lips, *mia bella.* I shall be imagining the feel of your naked skin next to mine—and I shall be cursing that infernal bell for not ringing a few minutes later, when I should have been safely inside you and when no power on earth could have separated us!'

The sexual boast should have horrified her, but it did no such thing. It started her pulse racing and that melting feeling came to the pit of her stomach again. But Natasha hid it with a look of outrage. Because anger was a lot safer than showing how vulnerable you felt inside.

'Will you take me in to dinner?' she said quietly.

Or *what?* he wondered. For a moment he was tempted to test her. But something in her eyes stopped him. A look which lit the light blue with a fierce kind of fire. He had seen that look before—it had been burning there on the night she'd walked into his life: a mixture of defiance and pride.

'Yes, I'll take you in to dinner,' he answered. 'But I cannot wait for it to be over!' His voice dropped to a husky promise. 'Because once it is over we both know what will happen.'

If it hasn't been for the brittle tension which

seemed to radiate from his powerful frame she might have challenged him on that—but she didn't dare. Not least because she was afraid that he was right and that she wasn't going to be able to resist him.

And since when had she treated her impending introduction to a Middle-Eastern potentate so casually? Had she completely lost her senses as well as her heart? 'What am I supposed to call the Sheikh?' she questioned anxiously, smoothing at her hair and wondering if it looked a complete mess.

'You can address him by his first name—once he gives you permission to do so.' He paused. 'And your hair looks wonderful.'

She pushed the remark aside as a servant suddenly materialised from one of the side-rooms, bowed and gestured that they should follow him. Natasha found herself wondering how much he had overheard as they climbed a staircase to the very top of the building. But all her doubts were dissolved when they walked onto the rooftop terrace and a scene awaited her which looked like something out of the *Arabian Nights*.

Polished lamps were burning and softly buffed bronze tables stood before low divans scattered with cushions in gold and burgundy and rich saffron. Beneath them the city lay spread out—the lighted bustle of the main square contrasting with the soaring floodlit monuments and the dark, twisting streets of the Souk. Above them was an indigo ceiling of star-studded sky, with a crescent moon shining like white-gold, and Natasha's impression was of so many different shades of light that she was dazzled by it all.

And then she heard the whisper of someone approaching and became aware of the focussed activity of yet more servants, trailing in the wake of the imperious character who now swept onto the terrace. He was clothed in shimmering robes and a headdress covered his autocratic head. The dark searchlight of his eyes swept over her, burning with curiosity.

Instinct told her to bow and then she raised her eyes and waited for the Sheikh to address her.

'And who is this?' Waving an imperious hand to dismiss the servants, he spoke to Raffaele, as if she had no voice of her own.

'This is Natasha.'

'Ah.' The Sheikh's eyes were like pieces of jet. 'Your fiancée?'

'Yes.'

The Sheikh surveyed her thoughtfully—as if, Natasha thought with slight indignation, she were some object for sale in the marketplace! But maybe that was how he'd been brought up to think, she reasoned.

'You realise how many women would long to be in your shoes?' he questioned softly.

'I count my blessings daily,' said Natasha demurely, and to her surprise, the Sheikh gave a shout of laughter, though Raffaele's eyes narrowed thoughtfully.

'And what of your sister?' questioned the Sheikh, his voice suddenly and unexpectedly soft. 'I understand from my aides that she is unwell?'

Raffaele nodded, acknowledging that this powerful ruler had some of the most thorough information-gatherers in the world. 'She is having the best treatment available—and now her doctors inform me that she is making good progress. I spoke to her this morning, and I haven't heard her sound so upbeat for a long time.'

The Sheikh nodded. 'That is excellent. Natasha—you must call me Zahid, not Highness. And now—let us be seated.' He flicked a look of barely veiled annoyance at a surprisingly modern watch, which seemed a little out of place when contrasted with his very regal and traditional robes. 'We cannot begin dinner until our final guest arrives, but we shall have something to drink in the meantime. You will take champagne, perhaps?'

Natasha shook her head, tempted, but knowing that she mustn't. She would need all wits about her if she was planning to resist Raffaele—and it was imperative for her sanity that she did. Her sensibilities must not be changed or softened by the introduction of alcohol.

'I would prefer something soft, if you have it… Zahid,' she said shyly.

Raffaele watched while Zahid beamed his approval and clapped his hands together in his most sheikish manner. Was Natasha just being extremely disingenuous—or was she aware that Zahid's upbringing meant that he rarely if ever took alcohol?

Or was she simply afraid of the effect that alcohol might have on *her* and her decision-making? Raffaele felt a beat of heat and of satisfaction. No. Not a drop of any intoxication had passed her lips when he had so very nearly made love to her in that darkened alcove before dinner.

A tray of heavy red goblets was carried in, and another containing small dishes of different nuts, and Raffaele watched with a mixture of bemusement and aching frustration as Natasha began to open up under Zahid's unusually gentle questioning.

He had never really seen her in this light before—but then, why would he have? Until recently he had never really looked at her at all—and, yet, now that fact seemed inconceivable. In her long gown she managed to look both modest and extremely sexy—but that shouldn't really surprise him, either. She was a woman in her twenties, with clear skin and sparkling eyes, her figure firm and fertile.

The ache inside him intensified, and suddenly it became about more than just fulfilling his sexual hunger. Raffaele found himself watching with something almost like *jealousy* as he saw Natasha smiling at a remark the Sheikh had made. Was the desert Prince flirting with her?

But, at that moment, the fourth guest arrived, and Raffaele rose to his feet, noticing that Zahid did not—that, in fact, he barely flicked the new arrival a glance.

The woman who entered noiselessly on sandalled feet was not the blonde goddess-type usually favoured by the Sheikh. Her hair was deep brown and her face pale.

Zahid looked up. 'You are late.'

The brunette shot him a reproving glance. 'Forgive me,' she said lightly. 'Zahid—aren't you going to introduce us?'

He frowned. 'This is Raffaele de Feretti, a business colleague, and his fiancée, Natasha—'

'Phillips,' butted in Natasha hastily realising that Raffaele probably didn't know.

Zahid nodded. 'This is Francesca.'

'Hello,' said Francesca, and smiled.

There was, Natasha realised, no explanation as to who Francesca was, or her relationship to Zahid. He hadn't even given Francesca's surname! But why would a sheikh need to explain himself if he didn't want to?

All Natasha knew was that Francesca appeared to be completely oblivious to Zahid's quietly simmering anger. Was he mad because she had been late, perhaps? Even Natasha knew that you were never supposed to arrive after a royal personage.

But Natasha's awareness of Zahid's displeasure was quickly displaced by her own growing feelings of confusion. On the one hand she was finding it ridiculously easy to converse with the eastern ruler and the enigmatic Francesca—but on the other she was becoming acutely aware of Raffaele watching her. And—try as she might—

she couldn't seem to stop her body from responding to that very calculated scrutiny.

Did he realise that he was making her skin tingle and her breasts feel heavy and aching? As if they wanted nothing more than to be touched and kissed by him. Did he know that he was awakening memories of the way he had made her feel when his lips and his hands had been familiarising themselves with her body? But even if he knew all *that* he would certainly not be aware of how he had captured her heart without even trying to.

She felt its beat quicken with the awareness that her love for him burned as strong as ever—but along with the raw sting of unwanted emotion came the equally insistent demands of her body, which were making her feel weak with unwelcome longing. She felt debilitated by it, as if she wanted to squirm and wriggle and have everyone in the room just disappear as if by magic and for Raffaele to stride over to her and pin her to the ground and…and…

Natasha hastily crossed one leg over the other—which wasn't terribly easy when you were sitting on a floor-cushion wearing a long dress.

But Raffaele knew of her agitation. She was certain of that, from the way those black eyes were silently sending her sizzling messages of sexual intent. The way that his teeth bit slowly down on the full cushion of his bottom lip. Did he realise that she was imagining him biting down onto *her* mouth in just the same way as that?

'Natasha? You will eat some of this mango sorbet?' asked Francesca. 'You've barely touched your supper.'

'Natasha has little appetite,' observed Raffaele softly, his black eyes alight with mischief. 'I wonder why.'

Aware that everyone was looking at her, Natasha took the dish that was being offered to her. At least the sorbet was deliciously icy—cooling down the heated clamour of her senses. She was acutely conscious of the fact that time was ticking away inexorably and that soon there would be no reason not to go back to the huge suite she was sharing with Raffaele. And then what?

Somehow she managed to get through the rest of the meal—nibbling at all the sweet delicacies which were brought in on beautiful dishes garnished with exotic flowers.

The Sheikh briefly shut his eyes, and Natasha thought how tired he looked. As if echoing her thoughts, Zahid rose to his feet. 'You will forgive me if I retire.' His black eyes were like chips of stone in the hawklike face as he glanced down at Francesca.

'Come,' he clipped out.

There was a momentary hesitation before Francesca stood up gracefully and gave Raffaele and Natasha a quick, forced smile.

'Excuse me,' she murmured, and then she too was gone, in a drift of filmy rose-pink fabric.

The silence seemed immense.

Natasha didn't know where to look, what to do, how to behave—but it seemed that Raffaele had no such reservations, for his movements were decisive.

Walking over to her, he bent to catch her hand in his, drawing it up to his mouth and touching his lips to her trembling fingers, his eyes never leaving her face.

'Bed, Tasha?' he questioned silkily.

Her heart thundered as he pulled her to her feet. Because, unless she decided to sleep *here*, it seemed she didn't really have any alternative. Were she and Francesca really the same woman—just a warm body suitable for the needs of a highly sexed and powerful man?

'Okay,' she said, trying to express a reluctance she couldn't seem to feel.

You don't have to do anything—not a single thing, she told herself fiercely, as she followed him down the seemingly endless staircase and back to their suite.

And the door closed softly behind them.

# CHAPTER ELEVEN

His black eyes narrowing, Raffaele observed the look on Natasha's face as she stared at him across the bedroom. No one would have believed that this was the same woman who had been gasping for pleasure in his arms earlier. Now she was watchful. Cautious. Her body language shrieking *Stay away!*

He gave a half-smile. 'Well, I don't know about you—but I'm exhausted.' Kicking off his shoes, he yawned and then headed towards his bathroom—but not before he had seen her fleeting expression of astonishment. The half-smile became even more wry. Did she really imagine that he was some kind of crass individual who would leap on her when she was very definitely sending out messages that she wanted no such thing?

But he was aching as he showered and he was

hard. He pulled on a pair of silk boxers and went back into the bedroom.

As he had suspected she would be, Natasha was already tucked up on one side of the huge bed, the linen sheet held up chastely to her chin, her eyes closed as she feigned sleep. He stood watching her for a moment.

'I know you're awake, *cara,*' he said softly. 'You want me to sleep on the divan?'

Natasha's eyes snapped open, and then she wished they hadn't—because the sight of Raffaele's honed olive body wearing nothing but a pair of shiny dark pants was playing havoc with her equilibrium. She'd never realised quite what a magnificently athletic physique he had—but why would she have? She'd never seen him practically naked before.

Yet, though she'd always been taught it was rude to stare, she couldn't seem to help herself, and it was impossible to tear her eyes away from the shafts of his powerful thighs, the broad shoulders and the perfectly defined chest.

His lips curved into a smile which was almost cruel, but the ache within in him was an exquisite agony. 'I asked you a question, *bella.*'

Natasha blinked, dazed by his proximity and the hammering of her heart. 'You...you did?'

'I asked whether you wanted me to sleep over there.' He glanced rather contemptuously at the velvet-covered divan.

Beneath the sheet, she shrugged her shoulders restlessly. 'It doesn't really seem fair, does it? I mean, it looks very uncomfortable.' She met the unhelpful look in his black eyes. 'Perhaps…'

'Perhaps, what? You're going to offer to sleep there instead? Is that it, *bella?*'

She eyed the vast space beside her nervously. 'Well, it's a big bed. Maybe…'

His black eyes narrowed. Was she really that naïve? 'You think so? No bed is big enough for a man and a woman if they are trying to deny themselves something they both want.'

'What are you saying, Raffaele?'

His mouth hardened. 'I'm saying that I won't touch you. At least not intentionally—not if that is what you have decided you now want. But if you press yourself close to me in the middle of the night and then claim you were 'asleep'—or if you clutch at me and afterwards assert that you were having some kind of bad dream—well, I cannot guarantee that I will respond in the way that a *gentleman* might.'

Beneath the Egyptian cotton her body shivered at the vivid images his silken words created. 'Wh-what are you saying, Raffaele?' she repeated shakily.

His black eyes were suddenly as hard and as obdurate as his body, and he wondered whether she was staring at him closely enough to see his arousal.

'I'm saying that I'm going to make love to you,' he said harshly. 'Unless you tell me emphatically that you don't want me to.'

There was a silence broken only by the faint cacophony of the distant sounds of the city.

Their eyes met. He didn't love her. He would never love her. A servant girl, the mother of an illegitimate child. Theirs was a relationship—if you could call it that—forged out of necessity. Only now it was threatening to spill over into desire…

Heartbreak, she kept telling herself over and over again—repeating it like a magic spell, like a mantra. Heartbreak.

Yet his dark eyes and hard body held a far greater lure than any spell, no matter how powerful it was—and all Natasha could think about was that she would never get another opportunity like this. That he would not ask her again. And could she honestly live the rest of her life knowing that she had been so close to the realisation of years of wistful daydreams and then turned her back on it?

'So, tell me you don't want me and let that be an end to it,' he asserted starkly.

There was silence for a moment.

'I can't do that.' Her voice was soft.

But he needed to be sure. He did not want her railing against him tomorrow morning simply because her conscience had got the better of her.

'Say it,' he commanded throatily.

Was this his victory, then, to make her beg? She swallowed. 'I want you.'

The ache within him intensified, but it was the honesty in her voice which moved him—so that the walk over to the bed where she lay felt somehow *significant*.

He shook his dark head very slightly, like a man emerging from the water and trying to rid himself of the last few drops. He really *had* been without a woman too long if that was the kind of bizarre interpretation he was putting on something so simple as having sex.

Yet it *had* been a long time; he could not deny that.

Why?

Because he had been working hard?

Well, yes—but that was nothing new.

Because there had been no one suitable?

Hardly. At any given moment of any given day Raffaele could have snapped his fingers and any number of beautiful women would have come running to him.

Maybe that was why. Because it all came a little too easily to him and he was bored, his appetite jaded by the inevitability of it all.

Yet Natasha hadn't exactly been unforthcoming, had she? As soon as he'd waved a credit card in her direction she had dazzled him with the green light. No one in their right mind could really accuse her of playing hard-to-get. So what was it?

He stared down at her, at where the shiny fall of her hair lay like a layer of honey-blonde satin over the crisp white pillow. Her eyes were the clear blue of an Italian spring morning and her skin like freshly poured cream.

Reaching down, he pulled the sheet away from her. She lay trembling in a satin night-gown as pale as her face, and he touched a little shoestring strap.

'Shall we take this off?'

Was this how clinical it was going to be? she wondered wildly. He'd strip her off and then presumably himself? So…so *mechanical?* She shook her head and saw him frown. 'No.'

'No?'

Would she sound ridiculously needy if she said it? But suddenly Natasha didn't care what she *sounded* like. This wasn't about her *image*, for heaven's sake, but the craving of her heart. And if this was to be the night she had long dreamed about then she wasn't going to be shy about conveying what her needs were.

'Kiss me first,' she whispered. 'Please. Just kiss me.'

'Kiss you?' Unexpectedly, he smiled then. 'Is that all?'

He bent down towards her, almost as if he was moving in slow motion, so that it seemed like an eternity before their lips connected. And when they did—well, for Natasha it was as all the books said it should be. A soft explosion, the awakening of a desire so immediate and so intense that she gave a cry of surrender and looped her arms around his neck, pulling him down to her, his hard chest crushing against the soft cushion of her breasts.

And Raffaele was startled by her sudden fervour, excited by the contradiction she presented—reserved and then passionate—and he found himself kissing her back with a fervour which matched hers, pulling her into his arms and tangling their limbs together. Only the slippery satin of his boxers and her nightgown lay between their nakedness and, yet, for once, he revelled in these sensual barriers.

Luxuriously, he ran his hands experimentally down over the silk-covered lines of her body, heard her gasp her pleasure.

And Natasha touched him back in a way she had never touched a man before—with a kind of delicious freedom and inhibition—and she rejoiced in the feel of his skin, the decadent sensation of hard muscle beneath honed flesh. Tracing the line of his arms and his thighs, she stroked the flat planes of his belly and the hard curves of his ribs.

Raffaele shuddered—because this felt almost *too* intimate. This was *Natasha,* for *Dio's* sake. Sweet, reliable little Natasha—who, it seemed, had become a sensual dynamo in his bed!

He groaned as he peeled the nightgown from her, tossing it aside as his gaze raked over her naked body and, as the night air washed over her skin, he saw her purely instinctive gesture of trying to cross her arms over her breasts. He stopped her.

'No, *mia bella,*' he husked softly. 'Do not be

shy—for shyness has no place between a man and a woman. Let me look at you. *Si.* Let me look at you. You are beautiful, do you know that?' he breathed. 'Very, very beautiful.'

Her skin was pale—so pale—and her breasts large, rose-tipped and, oh, so inviting. He gave an odd little cry as he bent his head to one and teased the tip with the soft graze of his teeth, and he heard *her* cry, felt her buck with pleasure beneath him as she clutched him even closer.

And then it was like performing an old, familiar dance but in a completely different way—as if someone had just shown him some brand-new moves. Was it because he knew her that it seemed so *strange*…so *distinctive?* Or because she knew *him?* For once, he could not hide behind the image he wanted to present to the particular woman who lay beneath him—because Natasha knew him through and through. She had seen him angry and sad—even vulnerable. She had seen him all ways.

He felt a stab of something—was it ire?—because in a way she was now seeing him stripped bare in every sense of the word. She would watch him lose control at the moment of orgasm—that one time when a man was as weak as he would ever be other than at the moment of death.

And Raffaele revelled in that sudden anger, because it meant that he could do what he was best at—giving a woman pleasure. He knew so well how to entice and to tantalise, when to advance and when to retreat. He knew all the places where she would be most sensitive.

He pleasured her with his hands and then with his mouth—a virtuoso at what he was doing—and it was with a kind of grim satisfaction that he heard the first of her cries as it ripped through the night air before he had even entered her.

But still he held back on his own satisfaction.

In the aftermath of orgasm Natasha lay reeling, her senses exploding—but she sensed tension in Raffaele, and she didn't know why. From being the man who had clearly wanted her—still wanted her—so badly, he had suddenly become shuttered, almost restrained.

Raising her dazed eyes to his, she brushed his mouth with her fingers and then she followed with her lips, coercing him into a deep and drugging kiss, willing him to let go, to relax. She felt the sigh and the breath and the tension leaving his tightly coiled body—heard the exclamation he made, something in Italian, and not something she recognised from years of hearing fragments of the language at odd moments.

Moving on top of her, he lifted his head and stared down at her for one long moment and then he held her face in his hands, as if he were framing a picture.

'Tasha,' he said simply, and entered her.

It was like nothing she had ever experienced. Ever.

It felt…*right*. Complete. As if the vital part of a jigsaw had just been found. Hadn't Raffaele said that himself earlier? But, of course, he had meant it purely in a physical sense, while, for Natasha, this was emotional. More than emotional. She opened her eyes to look into his before great waves of pleasure began to engulf her.

'Raffaele!' she sobbed, and then she felt him tense and begin to shudder within her.

His orgasm seemed to go on and on—tearing him apart with sheer delight—and afterwards he found himself gathering her into his arms and kissing the top of her head almost indulgently—as if *she* had done something special.

It was only when something unknown woke

him in the night that Raffaele was able to come to his senses. Silently, he slipped away from her, carefully disentangling the leg which was snuggled between his and then held his breath to see if she would waken. But she didn't. He pulled on a pair of jeans and a T-shirt and slipped out of the suite, noiselessly climbing the marble stairs to the terrace where they had eaten dinner the evening before.

It was one of those unforgettable panoramas which made you want to just rejoice in the very fact of being alive to see it—no matter how preoccupied you were. The stars were being swallowed up by the rose mist of the dawn sky, and he could see the dark blots of some unknown birds as they circled around a city which was still sleeping.

Raffaele stared out at the startlingly exotic skyline, where the tall, slender towers of the minarets rose up to gleam in stately splendour against the growing gold of the sunrise.

Well. He had done it. He had slept with Natasha and had probably had the most *fantastico* sex of his thirty-four years. He had gotten what he wanted—as he always did.

And now?

He leaned against the balustrade, barely

noticing the faint chill of the early morning air, or the coldness of the unforgiving marble against his bare feet.

Now—for the first time in his life—he wasn't sure. Had he been wrong to pursue something which he knew they had both been longing for? Should he have used his wider experience to call a halt to it before it had reached this stage? How was Natasha going to cope with what had happened?

Natasha.

Who would ever have imagined that she could be...

Shaking his head in slightly dazed disbelief, Raffaele gave a ragged sigh. Was it not just one of the exquisite ironies of life that a woman with the potential to be the perfect lover should be the one woman with whom it would be impossible to pursue a relationship?

But just thinking about her soft, scented body was enough to make him start hungering for her once more. He felt...*insatiable* around her. Or was that simply because he recognised that this particular affair had an exceptionally short shelf life?

Snaking his tongue around his bone-dry lips, he moved towards the stairs.

Decisions would wait. Everything would wait. And in the meantime he would wake her—in the most satisfying way possible.

# CHAPTER TWELVE

NATASHA stretched lazily, dreamily, indulgently—allowing herself a warm nestle into the mattress and an even warmer recollection of the night before. A warm, Moroccan night....

She blinked open her eyes and looked around, but there was no sign of Raffaele so, yawning, she sat up in bed and picked up her watch. Ten o'clock! Could she really have slept for that long?

Of course she could've. There had been very little in the way of sleep during the night itself. In fact, the whole weekend seemed to have gone by in a blur of slow, sensual nights and lazy, erotic mornings. And after breakfasting late they would set out to explore the city with Zahid and Francesca, and Natasha had wondered if there would be a tremendous fuss attached to being out and about with a royal personage. To her surprise there was not. But that was mainly on Zahid's insistence.

True, there were always a couple of body-guards hovering discreetly nearby—and they never had to queue!—but Zahid's flowing robes allowed him to blend easily into the background of the exotic city. Natasha wondered what the average tourist would say if they realised that a real-live sheikh was walking among them!

Drums and snake-charmers had provided background music as she had marvelled at the Badi Palace and the Saadian Tombs—at the souks and the astonishingly lush gardens which were unexpectedly dotted around the city. It was a place of smells and sounds and colours where Africa met an Arabian culture, all set against the backdrop of the snow-capped Atlas mountains.

After lunch they would return to the *riad,* where she and Raffaele would retire for their siesta—there seemed to be something so decadent and so wonderful about going to bed together during the afternoon so freely. And not just bed, either. The cushions which lay heaped in velvet and satin piles on the low divans provided soft havens for the slow thrust of their bodies, just as the cool marble of the floor contrasted so erotically with the heated softness of aroused flesh.

Why, once she had been leaning over to peer into the mirror and she had heard Raffaele move behind her. Jerking her head up, she had caught his look of sensual intent, had felt him exploring her, freeing her flesh. And, just like her, he had watched her reflection in the mirror, seen her pupils dilate in delighted pleasure as he had entered her.

Under his masterful tutelage Natasha had become bold, too—flowering beneath the exquisite fingers of her lover, feeling free and uninhibited enough to touch him as she had longed to for almost as long as she had known him.

What delight it brought her to see that hard and autocratic face soften beneath her lips. And to see him momentarily lose himself in that one sweet moment of release was quite something. *I could get quite used to this,* she thought.

A clatter shattered her indulgent reverie, and she looked up to see Raffaele walking into the room, carrying a tray with juice and coffee. He was already dressed and shaved, she noticed, his black hair still damp from the shower and a cream silk shirt clinging to the hard torso beneath. Natasha's heart turned over with love and longing.

Had this weekend changed anything? Did he

feel what she felt—that they had forged something between them, something real and unconnected to the reason which had initially brought them together? Was he ready to acknowledge it?

'Good morning,' she said shyly.

There was a pause. 'Hi.' He recognised the tone without surprise as he put the tray down just as he recognised the look on her face and, inwardly, he felt his heart sink. This was what women did. They were like fierce and demanding tigers in your bed, and then they turned coy. They wanted reassurance that you liked them just as much in the morning. That you wanted to take things to a different level.

But he knew from experience that he must be very careful. Too much reassurance always gave them the wrong idea—and he couldn't afford to do that. Not with Natasha—for hadn't he already broken every single rule in the book with her in these few days?

He put the tray down. 'Like some coffee?'

'I'd rather you came back to bed,' she said softly.

He gave a brittle smile, forcing himself to stay right where he was, even though his body was yearning for a little more of her sweetness.

'Well, I'm afraid you're going to be unlucky—I have a few phone calls to make before we leave for the airport,' he said obliquely.

It was as if reality had made an unexpected appearance ahead of schedule—the glass carriage becoming a pumpkin again before midnight had even struck.

'Phone calls?'

His eyes narrowed as he heard the note of objection in her voice, and he wondered if spending the weekend with a sheikh had somehow turned her head. What the hell did she think this was—some kind of honeymoon? Had she forgotten that this was all an elaborate ruse which just happened to have run away with itself because of a little sexual chemistry which he had foolishly encouraged?

His voice became stern. 'Actually, I *do* have to work, Natasha.'

'Of course you do,' she said quickly, and could feel herself slipping straight back into her old role. Obedient Natasha. Compliant Natasha.

Yet some cool new distance in his black eyes made her heart lurch with a nameless kind of dread. This wasn't how it was supposed to be. Not after what had happened between them. Because, surely, even Raffaele wouldn't deny that they had been amazing together? That what had started out as play-acting had become something quite different. Why, last night, in bed he had made her feel as if she was the only woman in the universe

But it was dark in the night, mocked a voice in her head, and you couldn't see his eyes then, could you? All you could feel was his body, and all you could hear were the things he was murmuring to you as he thrust into you—things he probably says every time he goes to bed with a new woman. What makes you think you're so different, Natasha? So special?

Taking the cup he brought over to her, she put it down quickly on the inlaid table beside the bed before he could notice that her hand had started trembling.

'I'll leave you to get dressed,' he said.

'Yes.'

He moved away from the bed and the distracting sight of her softly pink face, still flushed from sleep. 'We'll have breakfast on the terrace with Zahid and Francesca. I'll meet you up there. You can find it on your own by now, can't you?'

He just couldn't wait to get away, could he? 'I think I can just about manage without a map,' she said pleasantly—because she was damned if she was going to let him see her hurt and her anger. But it was mainly anger with herself that she felt—for allowing herself to *feel* hurt. Raffaele hadn't promised her anything, had he? Other than a great weekend and great sex? And he had certainly delivered *that*.

She forced a smile, noticing that he hadn't touched her. Not a kiss. A glance. A murmured comment. Not a single touch which might have made her feel she mattered.

She waited until he had gone before she drank her coffee and thought about how best to handle this. Now that they were preparing to return to England, Raffaele was clearly working hard to reestablish the boundaries and he had obviously decided that the whole bed thing had been a mistake. So she had some choices open to her.

She could seduce him—or beg him to make love to her.

Or she could keep her pride and her dignity and shrug her shoulders as if it didn't matter—even if her heart felt as if it was breaking into a thousand pieces.

There was no contest, really, was there?

She showered and dressed with particular care, recognising that make-up had another role to play other than that of accentuating a woman's good points. It became a mask you could hide behind—and she was in desperate need of some kind of camouflage this morning.

She chose a plain white silk shift which brushed the floor—the golden-ringed belt worn low on her hips its only adornment. Her hair she caught up into a twist on top of her head—simple and uncomplicated and the opposite to the writhing nest of emotion she was feeling inside.

But she wouldn't have been human if she hadn't felt nervous as she made her way up to the terrace, wondering what the day ahead would bring.

The two men were alone, standing overlooking the city, deep in conversation. When they looked up Natasha wondered if that was an odd kind of *guilt* she read in their faces—or was she now just getting paranoid?

But Zahid could pull charm out of the bag when he wanted to. Almost seeming to compensate for Raffaele's unmistakably cool body language, he bowed to her as if *she* were the royal—and clapped his hands so that servant after servant brought out different dishes of fruits and tiny little sweet pastries and strong, thick coffee in a beautiful silver pot.

With a start, Natasha realised how easily she had slipped into the role of mixing in such exalted circles.

'Where's Francesca?' she asked.

'She is in her room and, unfortunately, she will not be joining us,' said Zahid smoothly.

'Oh?' Natasha looked across at Raffaele, but his black eyes were as expressionless as those of a statue. 'That's a shame.'

'Indeed, it is,' said Zahid coolly. 'But she sends you her good wishes and says farewell. And I have told Raffaele that he must bring you to my country one day, whenever you wish it.'

'I think that Natasha is done with travelling for a while—aren't you, *cara?*'

Natasha nearly choked on a macadamia nut, but at least chewing it gave her something to focus on—something to stop her rage from bubbling to the surface. How dare he? How *dare* he treat her like some commodity he could just pick up and then put down again at will? Did he think she had no feelings? Or was he just afraid that she was about to start booking a two-week trip to Badr al Din, or wherever it was?

But pride was a funny thing—as soon as it was injured it began healing itself in order to protect. Thus it was pride which enabled her to smile widely at Zahid and to tell him how much she appreciated his kind offer. And pride which allowed her to tell him truthfully that she intended to come back to Morocco one day with her son.

'You have a son?' Zahid queried in amazement.

Which answered her unasked question of how much Raffaele had told the Sheikh about her. Nothing, it would seem.

'Yes, he's five.' She could see Zahid doing mental calculations in his head, so she cleared up any embarrassing confusion with the truth. 'I split up with his father when I was still pregnant.' Which would also, she guessed, make her a thoroughly unsuitable consort for the Sheikh's friend.

'Five?' breathed Zahid diplomatically. 'You must have been little more than a child yourself!'

Somehow she got through the rest of the meal—though that nut was destined to be the last morsel which passed her lips. She bade farewell to Zahid and, once he had swept from the terrace followed by a retinue of servants, she rose to her feet.

'What's the hurry?' questioned Raffaele, with a perfect view of her long legs from where he lay back against one of the stacked cushions.

'To pack, of course!'

Maybe it was because *he* liked to be in the driving seat that he now perversely found himself wanting to stay a little longer. Or maybe it had something to do with the morning sun illuminating her so that she looked like some glorious white and golden goddess. But she had turned her back on him almost deliberately and was walking away from him.

His mouth hardening with anticipation, he stood up and followed her all the way down the stairs until they were back in their suite, and then he caught hold of her and turned her round, a question in his dark eyes. 'Maybe we should delay our flight for a while,' he said huskily.

Heart pounding, Natasha stared up at him. 'Really? Why? What else did you have in mind?'

'That is a very loaded question, *cara*.' Snaking his hand around her waist, Raffaele smiled as he pulled her close into his body, his voice deepening as he lowered his lips to her neck, his eyes closing as he inhaled the delicate scent that was Natasha's alone—and so familiar to him. 'I can think of plenty of things I would like to do right now.'

And so could she. Things not entirely unrelated to his warm touch and the fact that she could feel the hardness of his arousal pressing against her, as well as sense the desire which thrummed in the air about them.

'Can you?' she questioned.

'Mmm.' He nuzzled at her ear. 'Can't you?'

'Raffaele, please—'

'Please, what, *cara?*'

She wanted to say *Please will you stop touching my breasts like that?* But it seemed that her body had other ideas—for it was revelling in the glory of his touch. Was it possible for a woman to know that something was wrong and yet to respond with a kind of unstoppable *greed?*

'Oh!' Her head fell back, her mouth opening in a gasp as he rucked the silk of her gown up around her thighs. He wasn't wasting any time with tenderness, she thought desperately. The golden belt had clunked its way to the ground, and now he was tugging at her panties, tearing at the delicate fabric impatiently. She gasped again—was it to protest at such arrogant disdain for the costly little piece of underwear? She would never know, because now he was touching her where she most liked to be touched, and he was doing it like a man on a sensual mission. And suddenly it was too late to do anything other than breathe his name out loud. 'Raffaele!'

'*Si,*' he said, frantically unzipping himself, levering her up against the wall. He stared down at her parted lips and huge dark eyes for one split second, before thrusting into her so long and deep that his sigh of satisfaction became a ragged and almost helpless groan.

There was no time to think, to speak, to object or even to kiss—because her orgasm happened so quickly and unexpectedly that Natasha felt almost cheated. As if he had robbed her of something and she couldn't quite work out what it was. And Raffaele shuddered within her almost immediately, his big body convulsing as he tightened his arms around her, saying something in Italian which sounded more like a curse than anything else.

She waited until he had stilled and then weakly pushed at his chest, appalled by the sheer *physicality* of the act. Her tongue snaked round her lips, her heart sinking with despair. He had *used* her—used her as a body, simply to satisfy his needs. *And you have used him,* taunted a voice in her head, and she flinched as she heard it.

'Tasha?' His breathing was steadier now, but his eyes were wary—because something about the intensity of what had just happened had taken him by surprise. 'Are you okay?'

She was far from okay. She was hurting like hell. But *signor* would never know that. 'Yes, I'm absolutely fine. Why wouldn't I be?' She opened her eyes very wide. 'And now I'd like to go to the airport and take a plane. Or is it *catch* a plane? I'm not sure. I'd never travelled by air before this—particularly not by private jet—but you're the expert, aren't you, Raffaele? You're the expert on pretty much everything. *You* tell me.'

He frowned and yawned, thinking that bed just might be the best option all round. 'I thought we were going to delay our flight?'

'But we don't need to anymore. Not now.' She moved away from him.

'What are you talking about?'

*Say it,* she told herself. Confront your worst fears and then they can have no power over you. 'Well, we've just had sex, haven't we? So we can leave right away. Unless you were planning to fit in another couple of bouts before we go back?'

'*Bouts?* This is not a boxing match we are talking about!' he flared. 'And there is no need to put it quite so…*clinically.*'

She stared at him in disbelief. 'Oh, please, Raffaele—let's not dress up the facts just to make them palatable! That's what this whole weekend was about, wasn't it? Sex—pure and simple—a basic human urge that we both satisfied. If that wasn't *clinical*, then I don't know what it was!'

'Why are you suddenly talking like this?' he demanded furiously.

Because she had suddenly come to her senses. 'Because it's the truth! You know it is!' And she turned away from him and ran into her dressing room before he could touch her again, recognising that this was not going to be easy.

Over the years she had learnt to love him—it had crept up on her almost without her noticing—and now she was going to have to *un*learn it. Because to Raffaele she was nothing other than a person who could be useful to him. She could perform a million roles—from making him soup and throwing the press off the trail of his sister to taking him in her mouth under the intimate cloak of the night and hearing him moan his fulfilment.

Biting her lip, she racked her brain as she raced through the possibilities open to her. Perhaps the only way she was going to come out of this with any degree of sanity was to revert back to what she really was. What she always had been. His employee—nothing more and nothing less.

She was hurriedly piling her delicate lingerie into a suitcase when Raffaele entered the suite. His attention was caught by the lacy thong which she clutched between her fingers and his mouth hardened.

'We need to discuss what we are going to do when we return to England,' he said curtly. 'Are you prepared to continue with this arrangement?'

Taking his statement at face value, she chose her words carefully, damned if she would give him the satisfaction of knowing just how vulnerable she felt inside.

She held up the heavy, cold weight of the diamond ring so that rainbow rays streamed from its faceted surface. 'For as long as we need to we will continue with this engagement,' she said. 'And, seeing as the press don't actually have access to the bedroom, they won't know that it isn't a proper relationship, will they? When Elisabetta is well and you decide that the charade is no longer necessary, then we'll just let it fizzle out all by itself. There'll be a new story by then and my debt to you will have been repaid.'

He stared at her, at an expression he had

never seen in her eyes before, and he couldn't quite work out what it was. A new coldness. All the habitual adoration flown. 'Is that how you see it? Is that how you regard all that has happened between us?' he demanded. 'As the repaying of a debt?'

Oh, how *arrogant,* she thought bitterly. And wouldn't he just love it if she told him that, no, he'd captured her heart into the bargain?

'Let's leave our egos out of it and just stick to facts, shall we, Raffaele?' she questioned coolly.

It was at moments like this that she took him completely off guard. For a moment, he thought—with something approaching admiration—she sounded exactly like his lawyer.

# CHAPTER THIRTEEN

HAD Raffaele thought that Natasha might relent on the journey back to London? That a hand splayed carelessly over the silken temptation of her thigh might have her breathlessly revealing that she couldn't wait to get home and into his bed?

In truth, yes, he had. But the reality was quite different.

She was cool, polite, distant. At first Raffaele let her get away with it—the flight was turbulent and there were too many stewardesses bobbing around and offering them unwanted glasses of champagne to challenge her resolution with seduction. But when they arrived back to an empty house and she jerked her head away from his slightly impatient kiss his eyes narrowed—at first with suspicion and then with barely suppressed anger.

'Are we going to stop this charade now? I think you have made your point, don't you, *cara?*'

'What point is it I'm supposed to be making, Raffaele?'

His eyes narrowed. How feminine introspection angered him! 'I don't know, *cara,*' he said silkily. 'And to be honest, I don't care—there is only one thing I care about right now, and we both know what that is.'

She stared at him, shivering at the cold detachment in his black eyes. How easy it would be to let him carry on kissing her—his sensual mouth and his practised hands stroking away any doubts she had. But how foolish, too. Every time he entered her body he was chaining himself a little more tightly to her heart. Every kiss was like a brand that nobody else could see but that was going to scar her for ever.

'I told you in Morocco that I will continue with our supposed engagement, but the sex stops. It…it has to,' she finished shakily.

'Do you want to tell me why?' he drawled, ignoring the sudden look of appeal in her eyes. 'Is it because Sam is due back?'

Natasha winced. He was concerned about practicalities, nothing more. 'In England we have an expression,' she said slowly, 'about not playing with fire because you only get your fingers burnt.'

His mouth curved into a cruel smile. As he bent his dark head closer he could see the instinctive tremble of her body, and temptation briefly flared. How easy it would be to make her take her words back—to have her pleading with him to make love to her. But Raffaele never begged. And neither would he waste his time with someone intent on games.

'Then, stay away from the fire,' he said mockingly. 'Let your body grow cold, instead, Tasha.'

Desire left his dark, rugged features as abruptly as if a switch had been turned off, and Natasha watched him walk away from her with a terrible feeling of foreboding. Wanting to call or to run after him, but knowing that if she did so she would be lost for ever.

'I'm flying to Paris,' he snarled.

'When?'

'Tonight.'

*Tonight?*

Sam arrived back from Serge's house full of energy and enthusiasm, and even *he* looked different—as if he had been parted from her for months rather than a few days. But being apart made you reevaluate things and look at them differently, Natasha realised. Yes, he had missed her—but only in the way a five-year-old boy *should* miss his mother.

I must make sure I never try to live my life through my son, she told herself fiercely. He mustn't become one of those only children of a single parent who feels responsible for the happiness of that parent. She needed to increase his freedom. She had to learn to let go. Of him and of so much more.

If anything had come out of this wild, tumultuous episode it was that lesson.

Once Raffaele rang from France. Natasha tried to convince herself that his clipped tone was due to the crackly international line, but deep in her heart she knew the real reason. Now that their brief sexual fling was over, he had distanced himself from her, and that, too, was inevitable. Yet, for the first time, Natasha recognised that by changing their relationship she had managed to destroy it. That there was no going back to where it had been.

Had she really thought that she could carry on like before after eveything they had shared together? With her serving him coffee and trying to forget all the achingly sensual intimacies they had shared?

At least, the news from the clinic was good. Elisabetta had put on weight and was benefiting hugely from the therapy. She was moving to a sister clinic in the United States, which would give her vast landscapes in an inaccessible place where no one would bother her. The world had moved on—a high-profile Hollywood divorce wiping away any interest in the half-sister of an Italian billionaire.

The 'engagement' was yesterday's news— even the huge diamond had taken to slipping round her finger so that it wasn't visible. The last two mornings she hadn't actually worn it, and nobody had noticed.

Usually, when Raffaele was away it just felt like a change of routine. This time it felt different. As if there was a huge hole in her life. Natasha couldn't settle to anything. She felt as if she no longer belonged—even the Italian she had been studying now seemed like a faintly ridiculous thing to be doing.

And what the hell was going to happen when Raffaele returned?

Something was going to have to give—and maybe this was the kick-start she needed. She thought about something Sam's headmaster had said to her when the exam results had come in, and made an appointment to see him before school ended.

The door slammed one evening the following week, and Natasha looked up, unprepared for the sight of Raffaele walking in, all windswept and sprinkled with droplets of rain, wearing a dark cashmere coat. That old rush of love came back—only, now it was sharper, stronger, honed by absence and the knowledge of his lips and his body and by a brief taste of what life would be like as Raffaele's woman. Her legs felt shaky as she watched him put down his briefcase, not daring to move or to speak for fear that she would do something humiliating—like beg him to kiss her, to take her upstairs to his bed.

Slowly, he took off his coat, thinking how pale she looked—all her old warmth and approachability gone. He stared at her. At the little pulse which was beating frantically at the base of her neck. He remembered kissing her there.

'How are you, Tasha?'

How formal he sounded. 'I'm fine. You? Good trip?'

'Productive,' he answered tersely, and turned away from the soft gleam of her lips.

He made a couple of calls and then went downstairs to the basement kitchen, where the old-fashioned range radiated warmth and a pot of something that smelt like stew was bubbling on top. Natasha looked up with the startled expression of a young animal which had just heard a threatening noise in the undergrowth.

'Would you like…coffee?'

She never usually asked. He shook his head. 'Actually, I need a drink.'

A drink? He never drank before dinner as a rule. 'You didn't tell me you were coming home.'

'You mean, warn you?' His smile was mirthless as he opened a bottle of wine and held it up to her in question. She shook her head. 'I thought I'd surprise you.'

Oh, but this was awful. Horrible. Like walking on something hopelessly fragile that you were afraid was going to be shattered beyond recognition if you took a wrong turn. She needed to act before that happened. 'Look, Raffaele, I need to talk to you.'

'What is it, Tasha?' he questioned, as he poured the wine and drank some, the rich vintage easing just a little of the tension which felt like a tight iron band clamped around his forehead.

'I've got some news.'

His fingers tightened around the glass and he put it down. 'You're not pregnant?'

She heard the horror which had frozen his voice, and its icy tone confirmed all her worst fears—made her realise that the decision she had reached was the best one for all of them.

'No, I'm not.' She blushed, furious with him for bringing the subject up when that was the last thing she wanted to talk about. She was trying to forget it. She *needed* to forget it. 'I'm on the pill.'

'Oh, come on—no contraceptive is fool-proof, *cara*. You, of all people, know that.' He saw the stricken look on her face. 'That was the wrong thing to say. I'm sorry.'

'No—please. Don't be. It's true, after all.' She had told herself that she wasn't going to run away from the truth anymore. So she wouldn't. She drew a deep breath. 'Look, I had a chat with Sam's headmaster the other day.'

'Really?' he queried politely, wondering if this was actually relevant. 'He's not in any kind of trouble, I hope?'

Natasha bristled. 'On the contrary. He's

doing exceptionally well. So well, in fact, that he's been offered a scholarship at a bigger school.' She paused. 'In Sussex.'

'Sussex?' he said blankly, ignoring her expression of maternal pride. His eyes narrowed. 'But that's miles away.'

'Yes, it is,' she agreed, her voice so bright that she felt it might crack under the strain. 'And it's beautiful. You should see the school. Right out in the country—they've got huge playing fields.'

'But you live *here,*' he objected. 'How the hell will he get to school? Or are you planning to board him?'

Over her dead body! 'No. He'll… Well, we'll…live in Sussex.'

There was a pause. *'We'll?'* he echoed softly. 'You're planning to buy somewhere down there, are you? Or to rent?'

Was he deliberately driving home her economic insecurity in order to make a point? To make her realise how dependent she was upon him? Well, she *wasn't!* Natasha drew her shoulders back, her earlier reservations melting away beneath the determined look she directed at him.

'Actually, neither. The school has offered me a job as Assistant Matron—and there's a little cottage in the grounds which goes with the post.

We can move in whenever we want before Christmas.' She took a deep breath to give her words real conviction. 'It'll be a fantastic place to spend Christmas.'

He was staring at her. 'You? Assistant *Matron?*' Raffaele's eyes narrowed. '*Madonna mia,* Tasha—that's a job for an old woman!'

'Actually, it's the perfect job for someone like me!' she retorted.

He wanted to grab hold of her, to haul her into his arms and demand that she stay. But maybe that was her objective. He stilled. Was it? Was this just another attempt at manipulation in his lifetime of women trying to get him to do what they wanted him to?

'Perhaps you are attempting to call my bluff,' he observed softly.

She stared at him and frowned. 'I'm not sure I understand…'

'Aren't you?' His mouth curved into a cruel smile as he observed how wonderful she looked—how glossy her carefully styled hair, how expensively creased the linen shirt she wore so easily with her skinny jeans. 'I suspect that you enjoyed all the luxuries that our phoney relationship brought with it, didn't you? Perhaps more than you could have ever anticipated? Maybe that's one of the real reasons you agreed so readily to have sex with me—why you slipped so easily and so comfortably into the role of fiancée.' His face darkened. 'But perhaps the outcome of our little *liaison* wasn't quite to your liking, *mia bella*—perhaps you wanted to go one stage further?'

'I don't know what you're talking about!'

'Don't you?' He gave a short laugh. 'I'm talking about marriage! Wouldn't it suit you better to give your role here some official status—as my wife? Hmm?' Arrogantly, he raised his dark brows, seeing the stain of colour which washed over her cheekbones. Was that guilt? 'And what better way of achieving that aim than by threatening to suddenly leave—with all the disruption that would bring.'

For a moment, she thought she might have misheard him. But the dark look of some unknown emotion on his cold face told her otherwise. She shook her head, her heart beating so fast that she seriously thought she might faint.

'How can you think that of me?' she breathed. 'How *can* you, Raffaele? To imagine me capable of such devious behaviour? I went to bed with you because I wanted to—because

I couldn't stop myself.' *Because I felt I would die if I didn't.* 'There was no ulterior motive.'

But he had been fighting himself and fighting the aspirations of women for too long to believe her. Had she imagined that he would beg her to stay? Would disclose that he needed her—he, who needed no one?

'Well, then, go, Tasha. Go and sublimate your own life and bury yourself away in some god-forsaken school somewhere.'

'As opposed to burying myself away here?' she questioned quietly.

He heard the accusation and deflected it back. 'That was your choice,' he said, his voice equally quiet.

Yes. He was right. Her life there had become what she had made it. She had settled herself into a predictable groove, perhaps hoping secretly that something would rocket her out of that comfortable existence. And something had.

Perhaps Raffaele's accusation was under-pinned with more truth than she had at first cared to admit—for hadn't there been a bit of her that had hoped for a storybook ending to the fairy-tale happiness she'd experienced in his arms?

Was this what was known as getting above your station? Had her head been turned by a hedonistic series of outings with a royal sheikh and his retinue? By her surprise ability to charm strangers at charity dinners?

She swallowed. 'How much…how much notice do you want?' she questioned.

'Go as soon as you want,' he snapped. 'I can phone an agency and have you replaced in an instant.'

Which showed her exactly how important she was to him. It was a sobering reminder, but perhaps a very necessary one. At least, she would be left with no illusions about Raffaele wanting her. 'Very well. I'll arrange it as quickly as possible.' She crossed the room to the door and when she reached it she hesitated, turning round to find him watching her, his face a mask of cold indifference. 'There's just one thing, Raffaele.'

'Yes? You'll need a reference, I imagine?'

Natasha felt dizzy, wondering if he was aware of the hurt he could wield. Was this how it all ended—nearly four years of closeness— with him offering to commit a few words about her to the page? But it hadn't been a *real* closeness they had shared, had it? More like her imagining of what closeness was. Because she didn't have any experience of it. Because she had wanted to feel close to him. But things in life didn't just happen because you wanted them to. Especially not love.

She nodded. 'Yes, obviously I'd like a reference—but I was actually thinking about Sam.'

Sam. For the first time the mask slipped—and Raffaele felt the harsh grit of regret stinging at his heart, because he had grown fond of the boy. 'What about him?' he questioned gruffly.

She opened her mouth to tell him that Sam was going to miss him, but changed her mind at the last minute. If she made too big a deal out of it wouldn't that be another accusation he might fling at her? That she was looking for a rich stepfather for her son? 'He's been very happy here,' she said. 'Thank you.'

The quiet dignity on her face made something twist inside him. *'Prego,'* he said harshly, and then turned his back on her and poured himself another drink.

# CHAPTER FOURTEEN

THE house seemed empty.

The house *was* empty.

Raffaele slammed the front door behind him and listened to the silence which seemed to settle down on him like a heavy blanket. Suddenly the silence was broken by the sound of carol singers outside. He flung the door open to see a *vario-pinto* bunch of boys standing on his doorstep, giving it everything they had—even though their voices were lusty rather than melodic. What was it, he wondered, that made Christmas songs so unbearably poignant when sung like this rather than in the perfect massed chorus of a formal choir?

Was it because they made him think of Sam?

And Tasha?

Tasha.

He narrowed his eyes as one of the boys held up a tin and rattled it. What on earth were they doing out at this time of night?

'Do your mothers know you're here?' he demanded.

'Yes, they do!' called a voice from the end of the path, and a young girl, scarcely out of her teens, came forward. 'I asked permission for them all, and it's fine. I'm the au pair,' she added helpfully.

She looked little more than a teenager herself, he thought, and he found himself staring at her. Natasha wouldn't have been very much older than this when she'd turned up that night. But that had been a long time ago now. She had been a big part of his life in that time—more than he'd realised—was it any wonder he missed her?

'What are you collecting money for?' he demanded.

'For orphans everywhere, sir!'

He withdrew a note from his pocket and stuffed it into the tin.

'Oh, *thank* you, sir!'

'Sing "Silent Night" will you?' he said quietly, and shut the door, wondering what kind of masochistic urge had made him ask for that—because it was so unbearably heartrending that he found he couldn't listen to it all the way through.

That evening he played opera while he was getting ready to go out—the most passionate and angry he could find—and found it as satisfying as it was possible to be satisfied by anything in his current state. He was due to attend a fund-raising dinner that he simply didn't feel he could get out of, though he had told the organiser to give his second ticket to someone else.

'You won't be bringing a guest, *Signor* de Feretti?' she had asked in surprise.

'No, I won't.'

He would leave as soon as it was reasonable to do so. Going was the last thing he wanted, or needed, but his company was making a sizeable donation and he knew that his presence was important to the charity.

There was the usual rag-bag of press hanging around the red carpet, and a couple of questions were flung his way about what had happened to his fiancée—but he gave a dismissive shake of his head and continued up the carpet.

Inside, he saw a few people he knew and many he'd done business with—including John Huntingdon, who had been there the night he'd taken Tasha to a dinner. He had a stunning and much younger woman on his arm, as usual.

Raffaele narrowed his eyes. Was it the same

one as last time? It was hard to tell. They all looked the same. 'I think we've met before?'

She shook her spun-sugar blonde hair and not a strand of it moved. 'Oh, no—I don't think so! I'd certainly have remembered *you!*' she trilled. 'Johnny and I have only been dating for two and a half weeks—haven't we, darling? Will you excuse me—I must just toddle off to the little girls' room and powder my nose!'

The two men watched her go.

'Your women get younger every day,' observed Raffaele.

'Oh, they're all interchangeable!' said John cheerfully. 'When you've been married as many times as I have it's as well not to foster dependence—far too expensive!' He frowned. 'But I liked that woman you brought with you last time, though. She was *different.*'

'Tasha?' Raffaele nodded, looking at the sea of glamour, the waves of silk and taffeta, hearing the trills of high, rather forced laughter. 'Yes,' he said slowly. 'She was certainly different.'

He thought about her all evening—and all night, too.

She had sent him her new address and telephone number, accompanied by a rather sweet little note from Sam, telling him that he was enjoying the country. And playing football. And somehow that had hurt as much as anything else.

Raffaele stared down at the winter-bare trees in the garden. Shouldn't he drive down there— take the boy a present for the holiday period? See what Tasha was up to? Would he ever be able to rid himself of this nagging disquiet if he didn't at least *try?*

The winter day was crisp and clear, with frost icing the hedgerows and fields and bright red berries daubing the holly trees and hawthorn bushes so that the landscape looked like a Christmas card. He drove past thatched cottages where trees twinkled in latticed bay windows and wreaths made out of ivy leaves lay hanging on glossy front doors.

The school had obviously been a stately home in a former life, because the approach to it was along a wide and winding gravel drive, through formal parkland. There was even a small lake around which padded a clutch of cold-looking ducks.

He hadn't told her he was coming. Maybe she wouldn't even be there. Why, there might even be some new man on the scene. Raffaele's mouth twisted and his leather-gloved fingers bit into the steering wheel of the powerful car. But why shouldn't she have a new man? She was in no way committed to *him*. Hadn't he made it starkly clear that he didn't want her?

An offshoot of the main drive curved away to the left, on it a sign saying Spring Cottage. As he approached he could see a figure in the garden, bending over and digging furiously and, even though the figure wore a woollen hat and unisex clothes, he knew immediately that it was Tasha.

She must have heard the sound of his car, for he saw her stop digging and straighten up, then stab the fork into the ground and lean on it as if for support.

Natasha stared. She didn't recognise the car—was it a new one?—but she didn't need to. Nor did she need to see the shadowed face of the man who drove it. She would have recognised Raffaele anywhere—sensed him at a hundred paces on a dark night, so attuned did she always seem to be to his presence. But that's because you're a well-trained worker, she told herself forcefully. Because that's what you spent all those years doing.

She watched as he climbed out of the car and began to walk towards her. His black hair gleamed in the crisp, clear light of the winter sun and his dark cashmere coat was softly familiar. But she didn't move forward to meet him. She couldn't. Her legs felt as if they had been planted into the hard and unforgiving soil which she had been trying to break up all morning.

As he approached she could feel the increased thundering of her heart. She tried to read the expression on his dark and autocratic features, but she couldn't. She wanted to drink in his beloved face, and yet she wanted to turn away from it—as if that might protect herself from the way he was making her feel.

She tried to smile, but the icy air seemed to freeze it onto her face and, inside, she felt the cold plunge in her heart as she realised how much she had missed him.

'Hello, Raffaele.'

'Hello, Tasha.'

They stood looking at one another.

'This is a…surprise.'

He nodded. 'Yes.'

'Would you…would you like to come inside?'

As opposed to standing here freezing? he wondered. He glanced at the ground, which was lying in great, dark chunks of earth—like giant pieces of the gingerbread she sometimes used to make.

'You're making plans for your garden?' he observed. And didn't that tell him something about her life here? She was settled. You didn't plant things unless you were planning to stick around long enough to watch them grow.

She wasn't going to tell him that gardening had become a kind of acceptable exercise and distraction therapy. That it helped break the constant thoughts of regret and the reflections which sometimes circled round and round in her head like killer-sharks who had scented fresh blood.

'I'm a bit of a novice,' she admitted. But then she remembered that last terrible conversation they'd had—which had started out with similar polite niceties and ended up with him accusing her of wanting to marry him because she had grown used to the luxury he could provide! You don't work for him anymore, she reminded herself. You don't have to be in thrall to him any longer. You're free. Even if you don't want to be. 'Raffaele, why are you here?'

The question—such an obvious one, too—completely threw him. He realised that he hadn't planned what he was going to say and that, for once in his life, his fluent and often acerbic tongue was not providing him with the perfect answer. Was that because there wasn't one?

'Weren't we going to go inside?'

Natasha shrugged. 'Okay.'

She pulled off her gloves and stuffed them in the pockets of her jacket, and he followed her inside, having to stoop his head to accommodate the low doorframe.

Once inside, she took her hat off, too—and he could see that the expensive blonde highlights had partially grown out. It should have looked ridiculous, but somehow it did not—because her hair had the natural gleam of good health, youth and vigour.

Raffaele looked around. Within the small cottage she had created the kind of homely nest which always seemed to spring up around her. There was soup cooking on the stove and drawings of Sam's pinned onto the front of the fridge. A simple little jug of twigs with some kind of furry tips had been stuck in the centre of a scrubbed wooden table, and next to the jug was an open textbook on French Grammar.

He looked at it, then at her. 'Given up on Italian, have you, Tasha?'

She was terribly afraid that she would do something stupid. Like cry. Like tell him how grey her life was now that he was no longer in it. Blinking furiously, she glared at him. Hadn't he got what he wanted—his pound of flesh and a couple of extra slices into the bargain?

'Why are you here?' she demanded.

'I've brought a Christmas present for Sam.'

'Oh.' Funny thing, human nature. You could tell yourself that you didn't want something—like Raffaele bringing up the thorny subject of their ill-fated liaison—and then find yourself bitterly disappointed when you got the very thing you'd wished for. 'That's nice.'

'He's not here?'

'No. He's out with a friend.'

'I see.' That was good. He wanted to see Sam. But not now. Definitely not now. And then he saw the expression in her eyes—that wary look, like a cornered animal—and Raffaele knew that he couldn't continue to keep playing it safe. He was known in the business world for being a risk-taker *par excellence*—since when had he ever played safe? But this felt different—and he couldn't, for the life of him, work out why. Because he had never had to take an emotional risk before? Or because he was seriously afraid that she might send him away? He drew a deep breath. 'I miss you, Tasha,' he said simply.

Her stupid, needy heart leapt as if someone had just made a loud noise behind her, but

Natasha kept her face neutral with the determination of self-protection. Did he think that she was some kind of toy? To be picked up and played with and then thrown away when he'd finished with her?

'Well, that's nice, too,' she said blandly. 'But I'm sure you must have found yourself a decent substitute by now. As I recall, you told me that all you had to do was just pick up the telephone and you'd have me replaced in an instant.'

He winced. Had he really said that? Yes, of course he had. And more. He'd been scared and he'd been angry—running from something that he'd spent his whole life running from. Imagining that all women were like the ones he'd been mixing with since he'd made his first million at an obscenely young age—grasping, greedy sexual predators. Unwilling and unable to believe that he might have discovered one who was unlike all the rest. Refusing to believe the evidence of his own eyes and his own heart.

He had convinced himself that her lowly position made her unsuitable to be his partner, but that too had been a convenient excuse to hide behind—because since when was Raffaele de Feretti ever constrained by convention?

He drew a deep breath. 'Tasha, listen to me. I miss you and I want you back,' he said.

Once she would have leapt like a starving sparrow on those few words, but Natasha had learnt a lot lately. Out of the bitter, broken nights of her heartbreak, and the tears stifled to spare her sleeping son, she had discovered a resilience and a strength which she would not let go of easily—for her sanity's sake, she couldn't afford to.

She smiled. 'There are other housekeepers, Raffaele.'

'I'm not looking for a housekeeper.'

'Really?' she said politely.

He looked at her with admiration. At the composure she wore like a mantle around her shoulders. Oh, but she was magnificent—how could he have spent so many years never realising that? Why, no other woman had ever faced him down like this—whoever would have predicted that Natasha Phillips should be the one who did? 'I am looking for a lover, *cara mia.*'

'Well, we both know there certainly isn't any shortage of candidates for that particular post!'

'But there's only one person who can properly fill it. You know there is,' he said softly. 'And that person is you.'

Of course her heart leapt again. And of course

she wanted to squeal with delight and run into his arms, and kiss him, and…and…

Natasha swallowed. This wasn't some game of emotional tennis with all the unspoken power which came from being seen to win. At the moment she held the upper hand. Raffaele probably only wanted her because she had taken the initiative and left before he'd had time to grow tired of her. He was looking for a lover, and she wasn't. Well, certainly not another lover like him—who could hurt her with the kind of pain she hadn't even realised existed.

'I can't operate in your world, Raffaele,' she told him truthfully. 'I can't do stuff like you. For you, I'm just another woman. But for me—' She stopped, aware that she was saying far too much—giving herself away when to do so would be to place herself in terrible danger.

He shook his dark head, the mask gone completely now, raw passion and truth burning unashamedly from the black eyes. 'But you're not just another woman, Tasha! You're the woman I want. The house isn't the same since you've gone—'

'Then, employ someone else! Someone else who will keep it cosy and warm and have pots bubbling on the stove, so you can fool yourself into thinking it's a real home!'

'That's not what I'm talking about and you know it!' he exploded, and he glared at her, raking his hand frustratedly back through his black hair. 'My life isn't the same without you, either.'

'But you're always going abroad!' she objected. 'I was hardly a day-to-day fixture. Your life can't have changed *that* much.'

'And I always used to come back to *you*,' he said stubbornly. 'Now I don't. You can argue with me all you like, Natasha—don't you think I've done the same, myself, over and over, to try to make some sense of all this?' he demanded. 'But the fact remains that I can't. I miss you. I want you.' There was a pause. 'I love you.'

And that stopped Natasha right in her tracks—because she knew enough about Raffaele to realise that he would never say something like that unless he meant it. He might be cold and cruel sometimes, and he had a reputation for ruthlessness in the business world—but he would run a mile from emotional blackmail and from using words that weren't true.

But he had said some awful things to her. Did he think he had the right to do that? That she would just let him? Wasn't it important to show him that if he really had changed, then so had she?

'You think that you can accuse me of trying to get you to the altar,' she said quietly, 'and then just pretend it never happened? As if it's okay to hurt someone?'

He held her gaze, wanting to hold *her,* praying that in a moment she would let him and yet recognising that if they were to have any kind of future as equals in an equal partnership he must let her wield her own power. 'I wish I could take the words back, *mia bella,* but I can't. I was scared of the way you were making me feel and that made me lash out. But I'm even more scared at the thought that I might have lost you. Me, who always thought of myself as fearless!'

He could see her lips soften, and the look in her eyes was telling him that the ice she had fashioned around her heart was slowly melting away. How easy it would be to take her in his arms now, he thought, and to coax her answer from her with his lips.

But this was too important to be dictated by desire.

He played his trump card. 'The question is whether or not you can look into my eyes and tell me that you don't love me. Can you do that, Tasha? Can you honestly do that?'

She looked at him then, and the last of the fight went out of her. 'You know I can't,' she whispered. 'You've known that all along.'

Briefly, he closed his eyes and, when he opened them again, he held out his arms to her. 'Come here. Come to me, Tasha.'

She hesitated for one last, unwanted second before she went into them—like someone who had been standing frozen outside for too long. She had to bite her lip to stop the tears. 'Oh, Raffaele!'

She was shaking, and Raffaele tenderly kissed away the tears which had begun to slide down her face despite all her best intentions. He pulled her closer and held her tightly, and they stayed just like that for a long time, before he bent his mouth to her ear, his breath warm against her silken hair.

'Now, take me bed,' he whispered. 'For I will not wait a moment longer.'

'Oh, won't you?' she teased. But Natasha felt newly powerful as she led him into her tiny room, even when he took one look at her narrow bed and started laughing.

'*Dios!*' he exclaimed in a low voice. 'I do not think that I have slept on such a bed since I was ten!'

'I didn't think you were planning on doing much sleeping,' she said, both confident and yet strangely shy in light of the look he was now slanting over her.

'Ah, Tasha,' he whispered tenderly, and touched her cheek, brushing away a smudge of mud with the pad of his thumb. 'Look at you. *Bella. Mia bella—sempre.*' And then his voice suddenly became urgent, sharpened by the thought of what he had so nearly lost. 'Kiss me,' he demanded. 'Kiss me now.'

Rising up on tiptoe, she wound her arms around his neck and put her lips to his. He made a little groan of delight, and she found herself smiling through the passion—because she could make this incredible man moan with just a kiss.

It was too cold in the small cottage for a leisurely undressing, and their clothes ended up in a heap on the bedroom floor—Natasha's gardening trousers strewn over Raffaele's cashmere sweater. In the confined space they lay close together under the duvet, exploring each other with eyes and lips and hands as if it was the first time.

And in a way it was—certainly for Raffaele. The first time he'd ever had sex and allowed— no, *wanted*—emotion to enter into the equation.

So that afterwards he was dazed, shaken, pulling her into his hard body, his embrace fierce, possessive, protective as their heartbeats stilled.

And later they lit a fire and sat on the floor in front of it while they roasted the chestnuts she'd bought yesterday at the market—and that was where Sam found them.

He took one look at them and a smile like the sun broke out on his face—then he gave a little squeal and hurled himself into Raffaele's arms.

# EPILOGUE

IT HAD been—as Natasha said—the worst possible time for a man to turn up on her doorstep and tell her that he wanted to spend the rest of his life with her. She had, after all, just taken on a new job and Sam was due to start at the school after the Christmas holidays.

Raffaele had bitten back his instinctive demand that she go with him instantly, recognising that Tasha's dislike of letting anybody down was one of the things he loved about her. He gave a slow smile of contentment. There were so many!

So they had sat Sam down and asked him what *he* wanted to do—but his answer hadn't really helped, since he'd told them that he didn't care where they lived just as long as the three of them were together.

And, in that moment, Natasha had recognised that Raffaele was a hugely influential force in her son's life—that he was a father to Sam in almost every sense of the word. Sam had been missing him, too, she realised.

In the end they had gone to see the head-teacher and explained their predicament.

She had looked at Natasha with a stern expression. 'I can't say I'm not disappointed,' she'd said. 'Because I am.'

Then she'd looked at Raffaele. 'And I can't say I'm surprised, either,' she'd added softly, her face softening.

Raffaele had smiled. 'Thank you. But we've decided that we'd like Sam to come to school here, anyway. We're going to buy a house nearby.'

'Oh, you *are?* Oh, that's wonderful!'

The head had beamed and sent for tea, and afterwards Raffaele told Tasha that he had felt about ten years old, sitting in that study! Once, he would have gone to hell and back rather than make such an admission. But that was one of the greatest things about love—it liberated you in so many ways.

And with the whole world to choose from the two of them had fallen in love with this corner of the English countryside. It was close enough to a major airport for Raffaele to take trips abroad—even though the lure of travel was palling and, for the first time in his life, he could see the attraction of being successful enough to delegate and stay home more. It was also close enough for him to travel into London as often as he wanted—he could do what many other businessmen did these days, which was to fly in by helicopter.

They had found a big old house in a decent-sized plot—with a garden big enough for Sam to have an entire junior football match on if he wanted to. There were stables for the horses that Natasha had always had a yearning to ride, and a flint-walled kitchen garden which got just enough summer sun to provide the white peaches which Raffaele had adored when he was a little boy. They might not grow as big nor quite as sweet as those remembered fruits—but growing them would be a symbol of something he had found with Tasha. Roots.

It was the kind of house that neither of them had ever had but both had longed for. It was a home, in fact. Their first real home.

'Home is where the heart is,' said Natasha, as he touched his lips to hers before carrying her over the threshold and continuing straight upstairs towards their bedroom. 'Corny, but true.'

He could feel his own heart's thundering beat

and his body's urgent need to join with hers. 'Then my home is with you, *mia bella,*' he said softly. *'Per sempre.'*

Natasha's Italian had come on well enough for her to know that this meant *always*—but even if she hadn't spoken a word of the language she would have understood what he meant.

She could read it in his eyes.

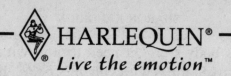

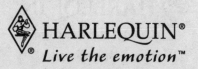

# HARLEQUIN®
# INTRIGUE®

## BREATHTAKING ROMANTIC SUSPENSE

Shared dangers and passions lead to electrifying
romance and heart-stopping suspense!

Every month, you'll meet six new heroes
who are guaranteed to make your spine tingle
and your pulse pound. With them you'll enter
into the exciting world of Harlequin Intrigue—
where your life is on the line
and so is your heart!

## THAT'S INTRIGUE— ROMANTIC SUSPENSE AT ITS BEST!

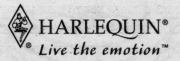

## Harlequin® Historical
### Historical Romantic Adventure!

*Imagine a time of chivalrous
knights and unconventional ladies,
roguish rakes and impetuous
heiresses, rugged cowboys
and spirited frontierswomen—
these rich and vivid tales will
capture your imagination!*

*Harlequin Historical . . .
they're too good to miss!*